2023

I hope you have a
and Merry Christmas!
My Warmest Regards,
[illegible signature]

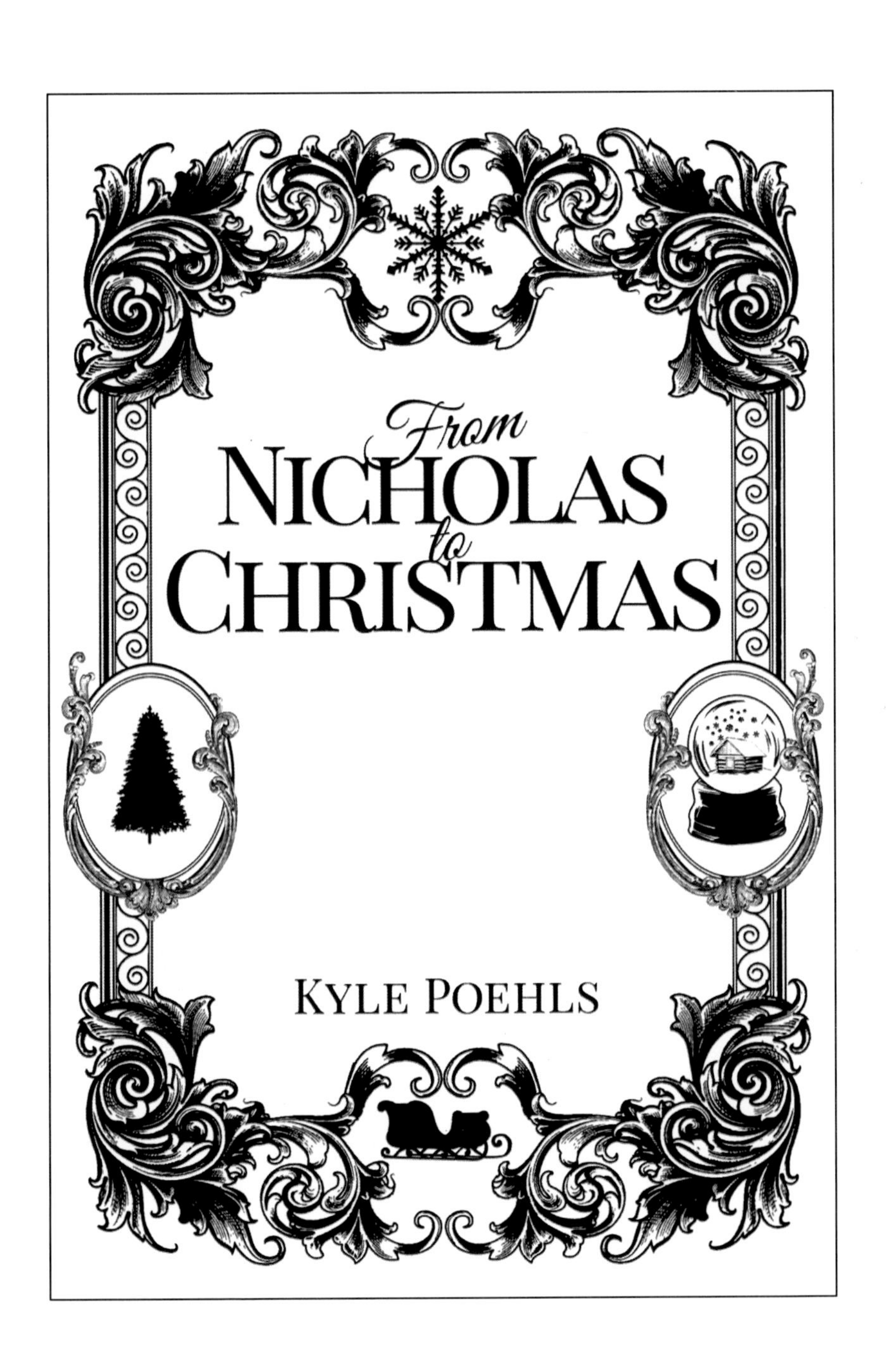

From Nicholas *to* Christmas

Kyle Poehls

This is a work of fiction. All of the names, characters, organizations, and incidents are the product of the author's imagination or are used fictitiously.

FROM NICHOLAS TO CHRISTMAS

Library of Congress Cataloging-in-Publication Data

Names: Poehls, Kyle – author.
Title: From Nicholas To Christmas / Kyle Poehls
Identifiers: LCCN 2020910565 |
ISBN 978-1-7352076-0-5 (Hardcover) | 978-1-7352076-1-2 (eBook)

Subjects: | GSAFD: Fables
Published By: North Poehls Arts, LLC.

Printed in the United States of America.

First Edition: 2020

10 9 8 7 6 5 4 3 2 1

For the spirit of the season
to last for every age

Acknowledgements

First and foremost, this book and dream would never have been possible if it weren't for the efforts and support given when my life was on the line: to Kari, my parents, to Dr. Joseph Brown and the medical staff at Walter Reed National Military Medical Center, to Brent, and finally to the others who made visits during my hospitalizations.

To my wife, Kari: thank you for all your love and care since the first day I met you, and the endless hours you've spent by my side. I love you with all my heart!

To my parents, Roger and Cheryl: I couldn't have asked for better parents. My principles and values were developed and mirrored from you two, and there's no thanks that could ever repay that gift.

To Brent Olsson: a person who embodies the expression "you don't have to be related to be family." You've been a brother to me for as long as we've known each other. Thank you for always being there.

To Dr. Joseph Brown: twice you've saved my life! I honestly don't know what else I could put down in this portion that could show my gratitude and thanks any more. You and the medical staff at Walter Reed in charge of my case showed a level of care, patience and support unmatched by anything I have ever seen.

To my editor, Debra L. Hartmann at theprobookeditor.com: what an excellent job you did! Working with you was such an effortless process, and I couldn't have asked for an editor who offered such amazing guidance and editorial expertise on this book.

Finally. to my illustrator, Diego: my time with you was fantastic. Your patience and openness to *any* small changes requested made the experience phenomenal with you. I hope everyone can get the chance to look at your work on your Instagram page at http://instagram.com/dieguitoli or website at dieguitoli.com.

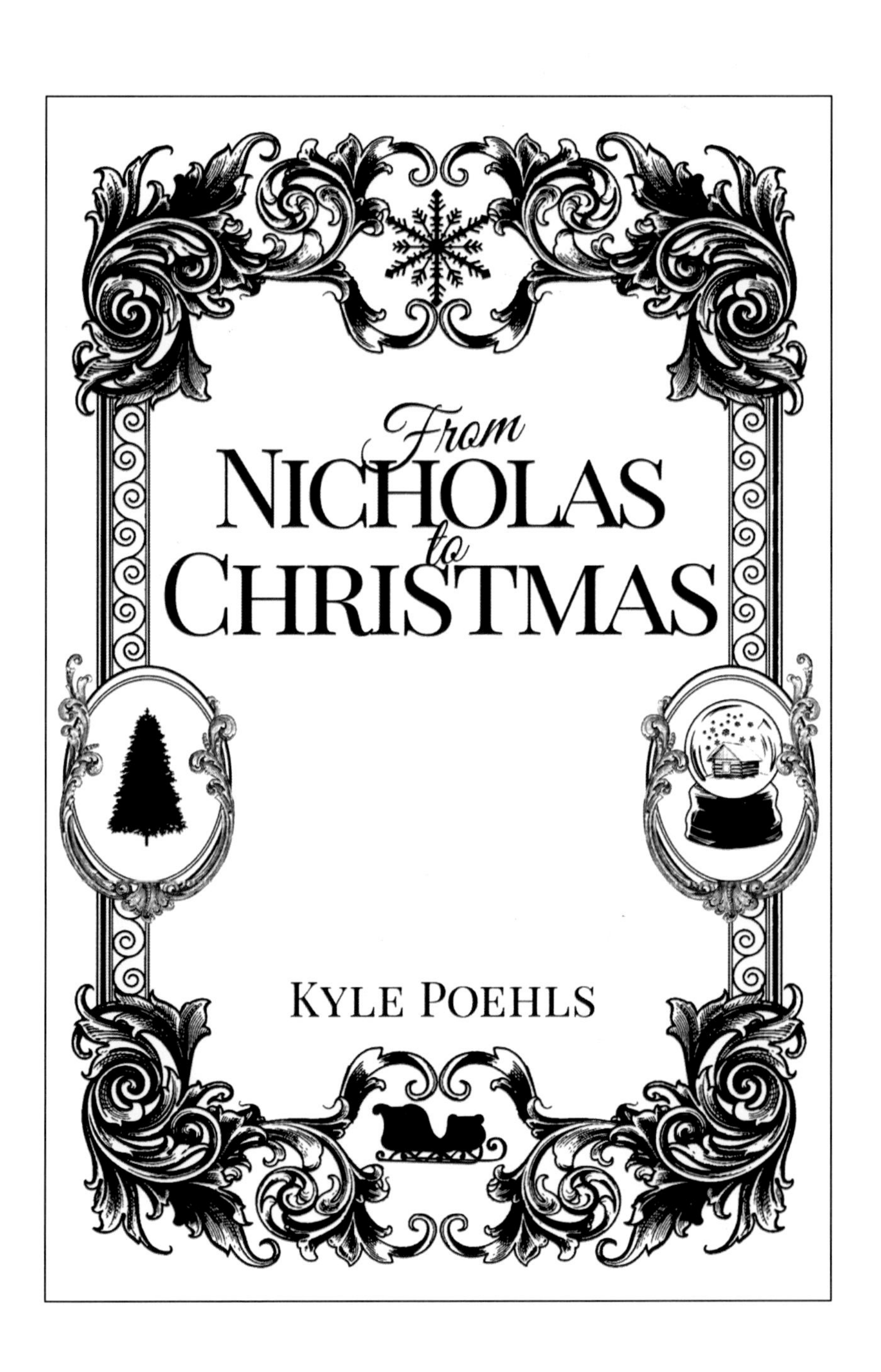

From NICHOLAS *to* CHRISTMAS

KYLE POEHLS

PART ONE
MEETING NICHOLAS

"Christmas will always be
as long as we stand heart-to-heart
and hand-in-hand"

- Dr. Seuss -

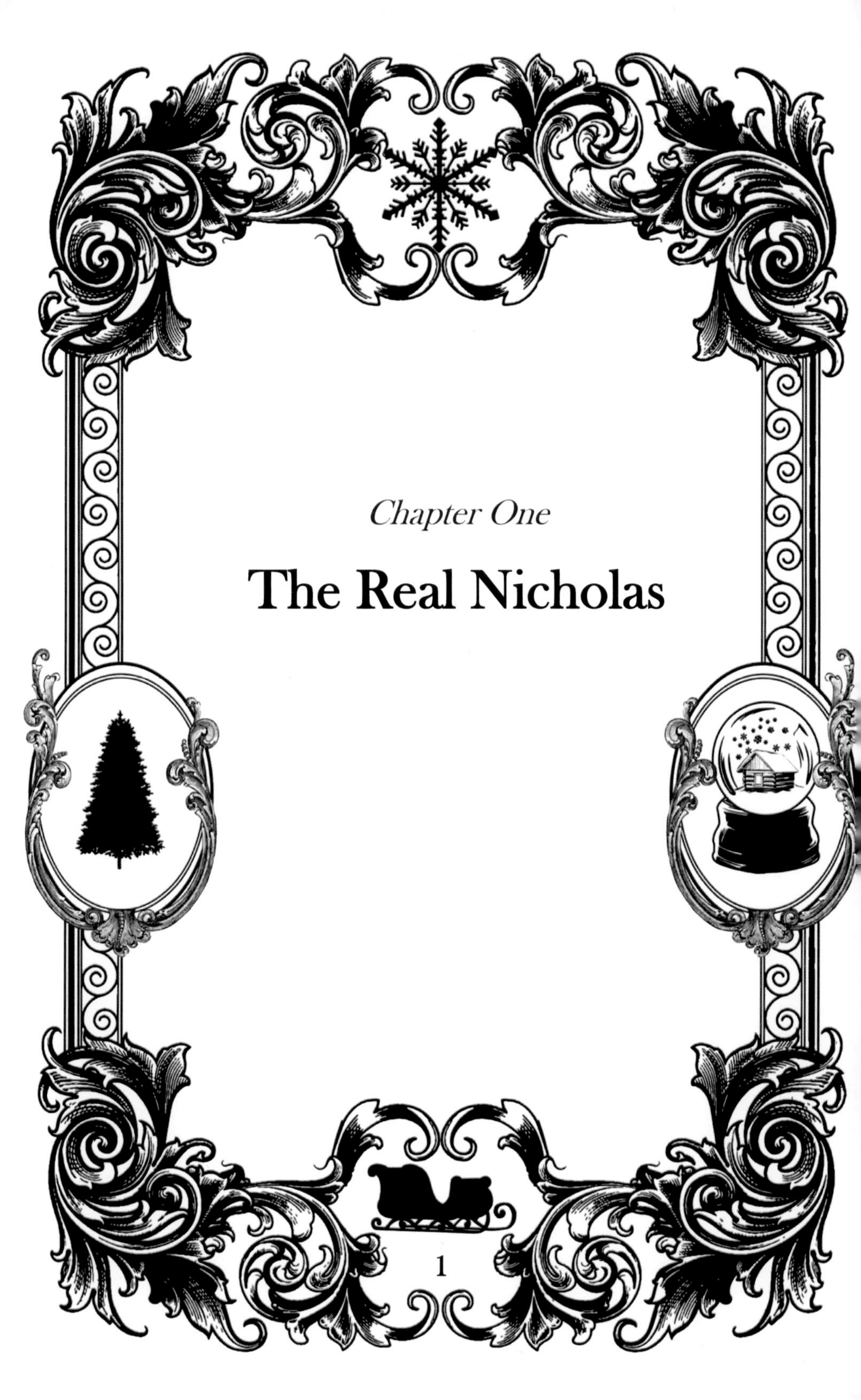

Chapter One

The Real Nicholas

A crunch of the snow was the
sound in the night;
Then Nicholas and all
emerged into sight.

His two little children were
following in tow;
Just helping their father drag
wood through the snow

It's said he is magic for what
he can do;
And that he may visit, leaving
no sign or clue.

All tales and his stories
changed more over time;
Making myths out of air and
his songs into rhymes.

But this one is different, and
now you will see;
When Nicholas was just
Nicholas, before Christmas
came to be.

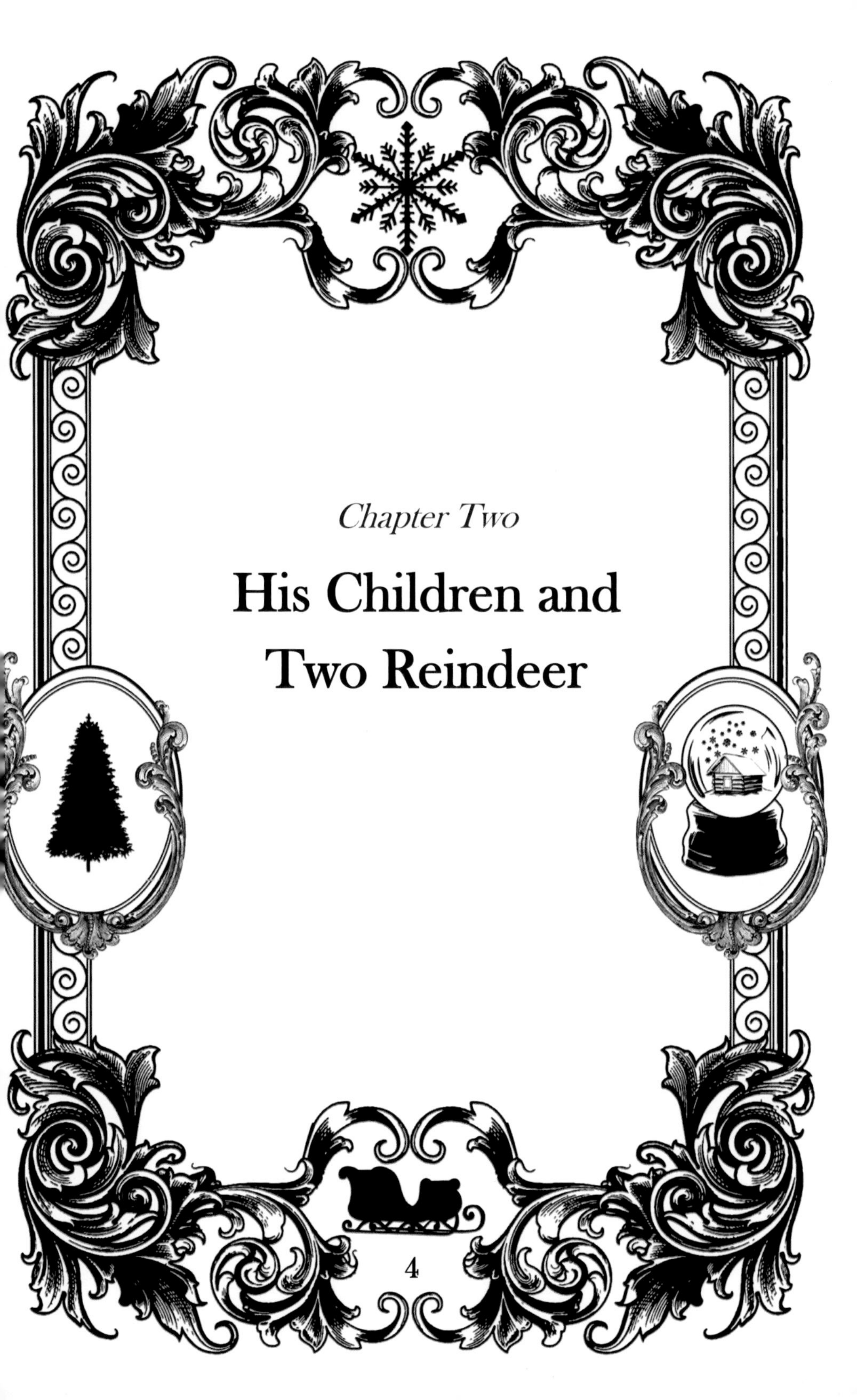

Chapter Two

His Children and Two Reindeer

It started one night, which
begins this whole tale;
With him and his helpers all
walking a trail.

Holly and Timmy went with
him that day;
While Donner and Vixen
pulled Nicholas's sleigh.

His children helped out
wherever they could;
With the other two pulling a
cart full of wood.

They went to the forest to
gather supplies;
For Nicholas to build things of
all shapes and size.

The trees, with their wood,
are all that he needs;
To work for a living and do
some good deeds.

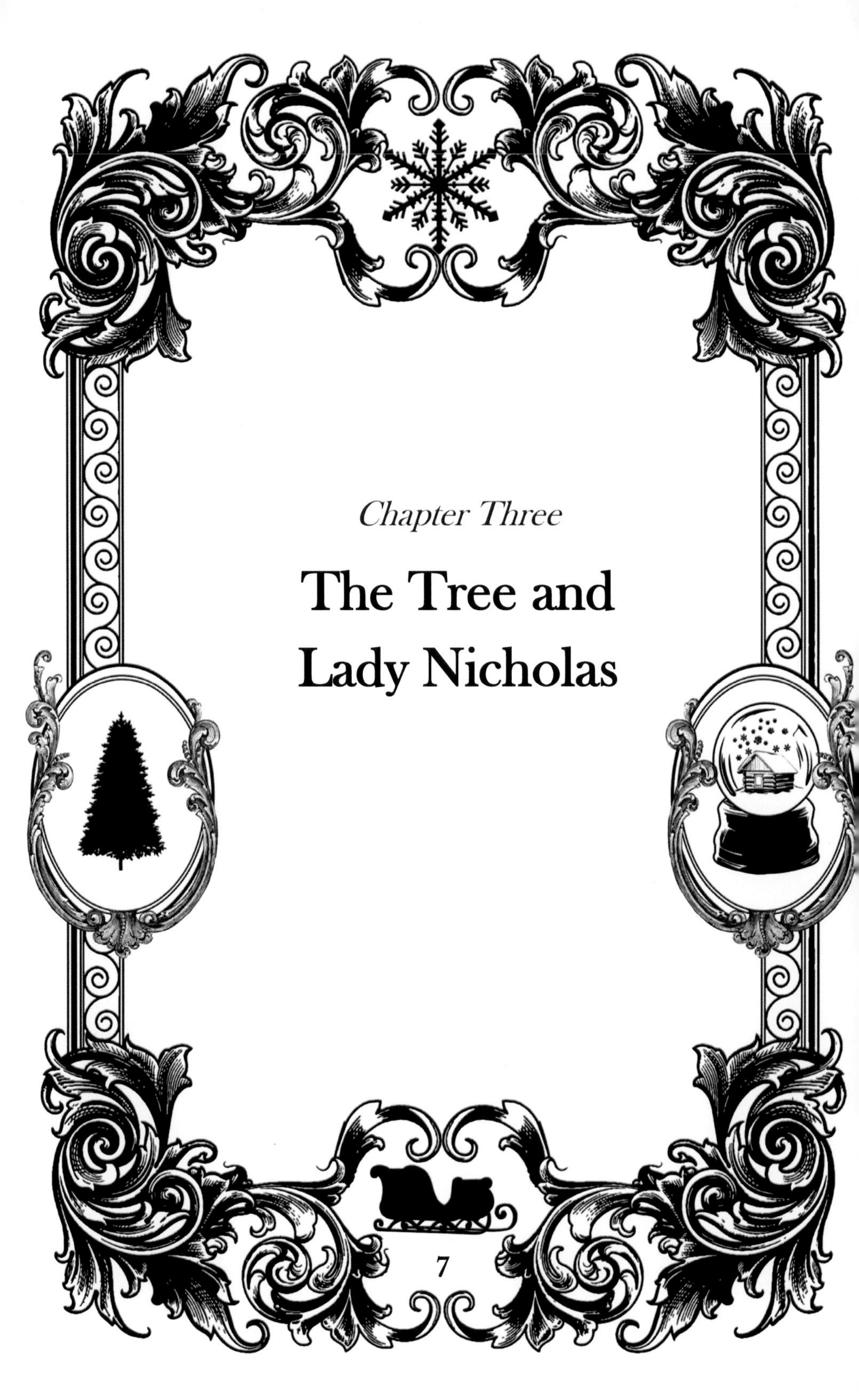

Chapter Three

The Tree and Lady Nicholas

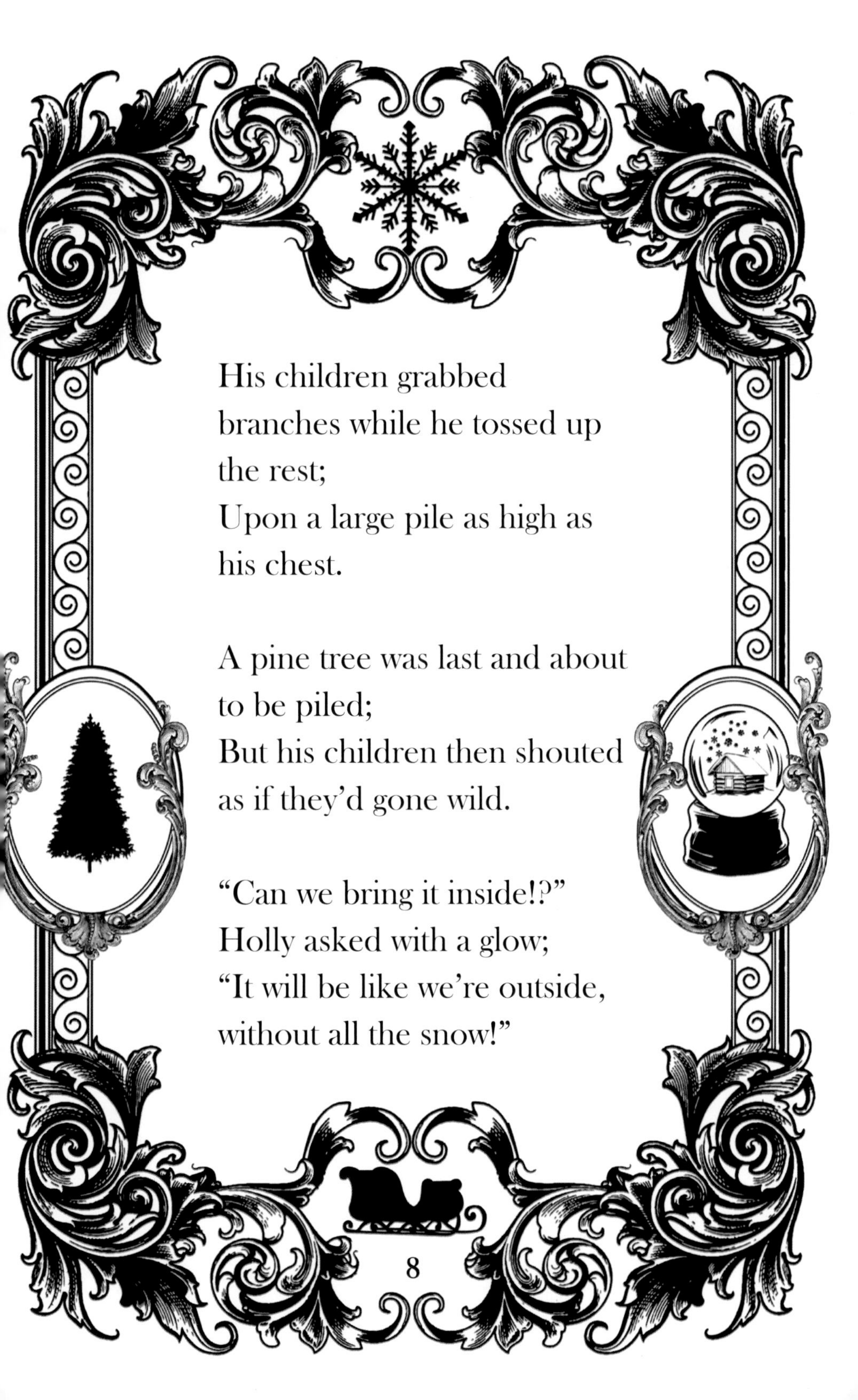

His children grabbed branches while he tossed up the rest;
Upon a large pile as high as his chest.

A pine tree was last and about to be piled;
But his children then shouted as if they'd gone wild.

"Can we bring it inside!?" Holly asked with a glow;
"It will be like we're outside, without all the snow!"

"Of course!" he responded
and stood it up tall;
Then led the two reindeer
inside the barn stall.

Holly and Timmy raced
toward the front door;
To Mom's open arms and a
warm fire's roar.

As Donner and Vixen were
tucked for the night;
Nicholas picked up his bag
and he blew out the light.

Then, he walked through the
snow with that tree in his hand;
Leaving paths of green thistles
on snow-covered land.

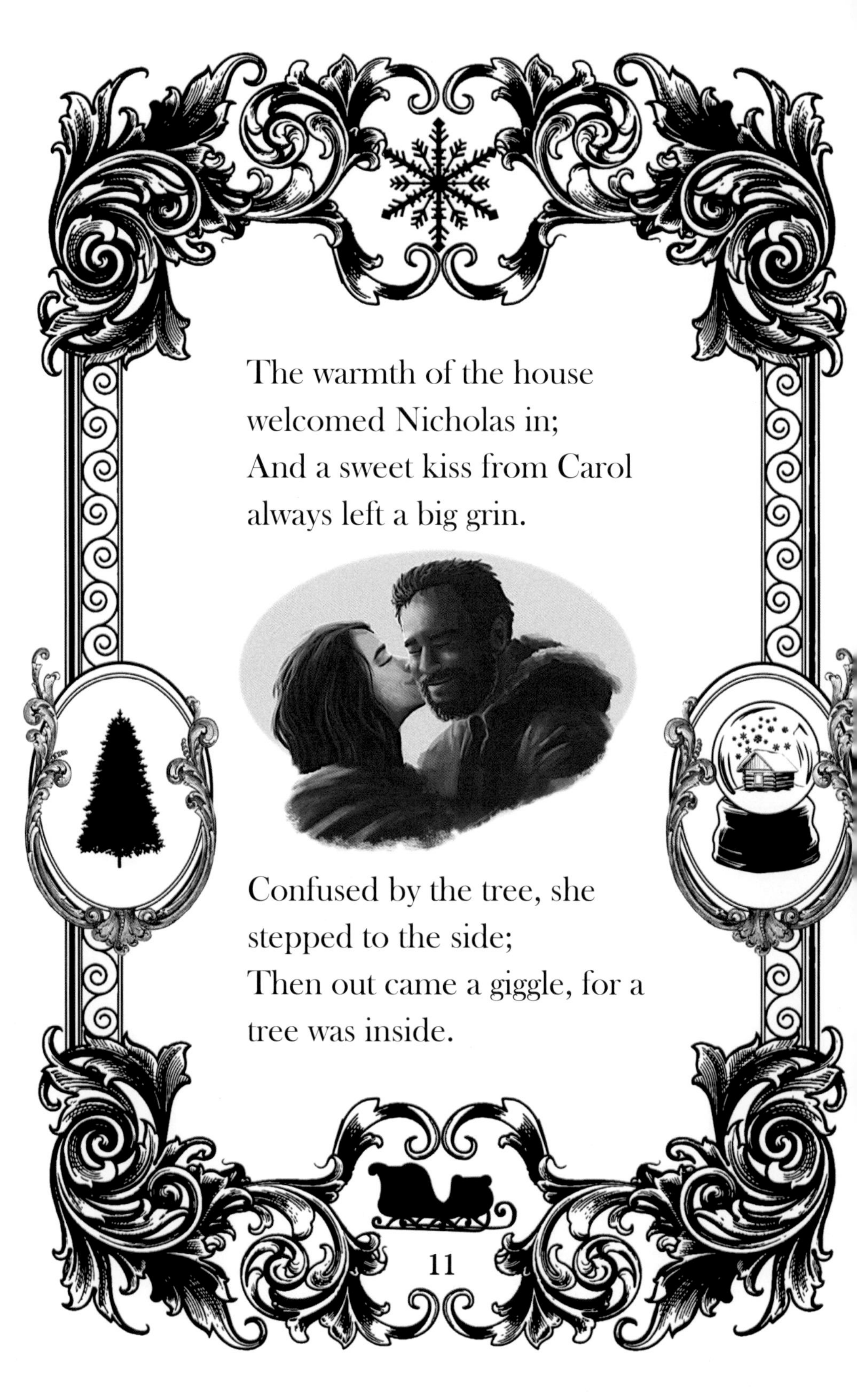

The warmth of the house
welcomed Nicholas in;
And a sweet kiss from Carol
always left a big grin.

Confused by the tree, she
stepped to the side;
Then out came a giggle, for a
tree was inside.

He walked to the corner while carrying that tree;
To a spot in the house where all eyes could see.

The children were digging, around and about;
For toys in the chest, to lay them all out.

There were houses and
people, and *even* a cow;
Either laid on the ground or
strung on a bough.

The laughter and joy were
nothing to stop;
But something had happened,
which made their jaw drop.

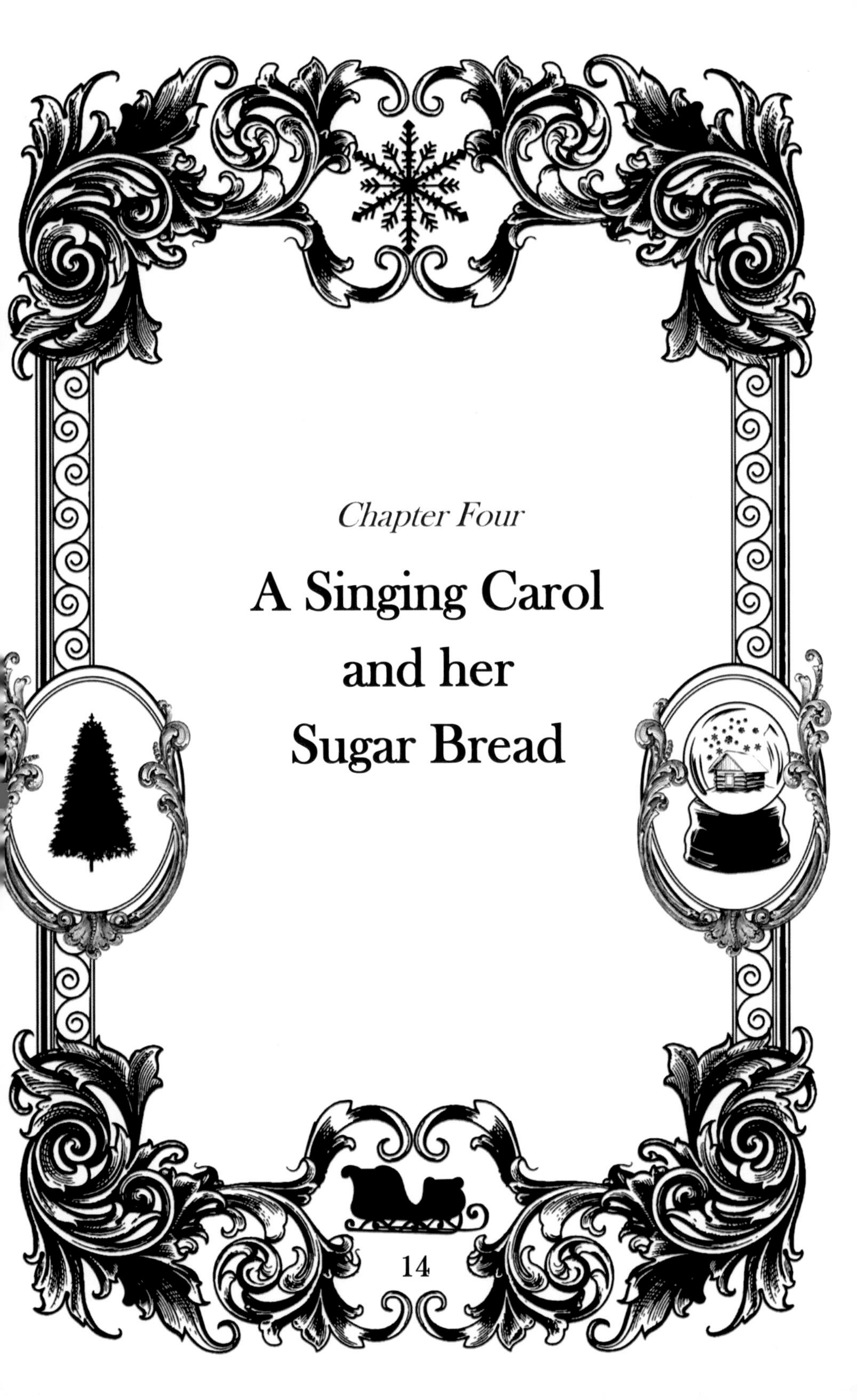

Chapter Four

A Singing Carol and her Sugar Bread

They saw what was baking and
later would eat;
It was bread topped with sugar
and deliciously sweet.

She baked it just right,
where it was soft from within;
So crispy and buttery, it would
make your head spin.

A song then arose, with a stir here and there;
She whispered at first, then she filled up the air.

Her voice gave a warmth and a beautiful sound;
That would make scrooges give and then dance all around.

With cooking now finished,
they each took a seat;
But had to do one thing
before they could eat.

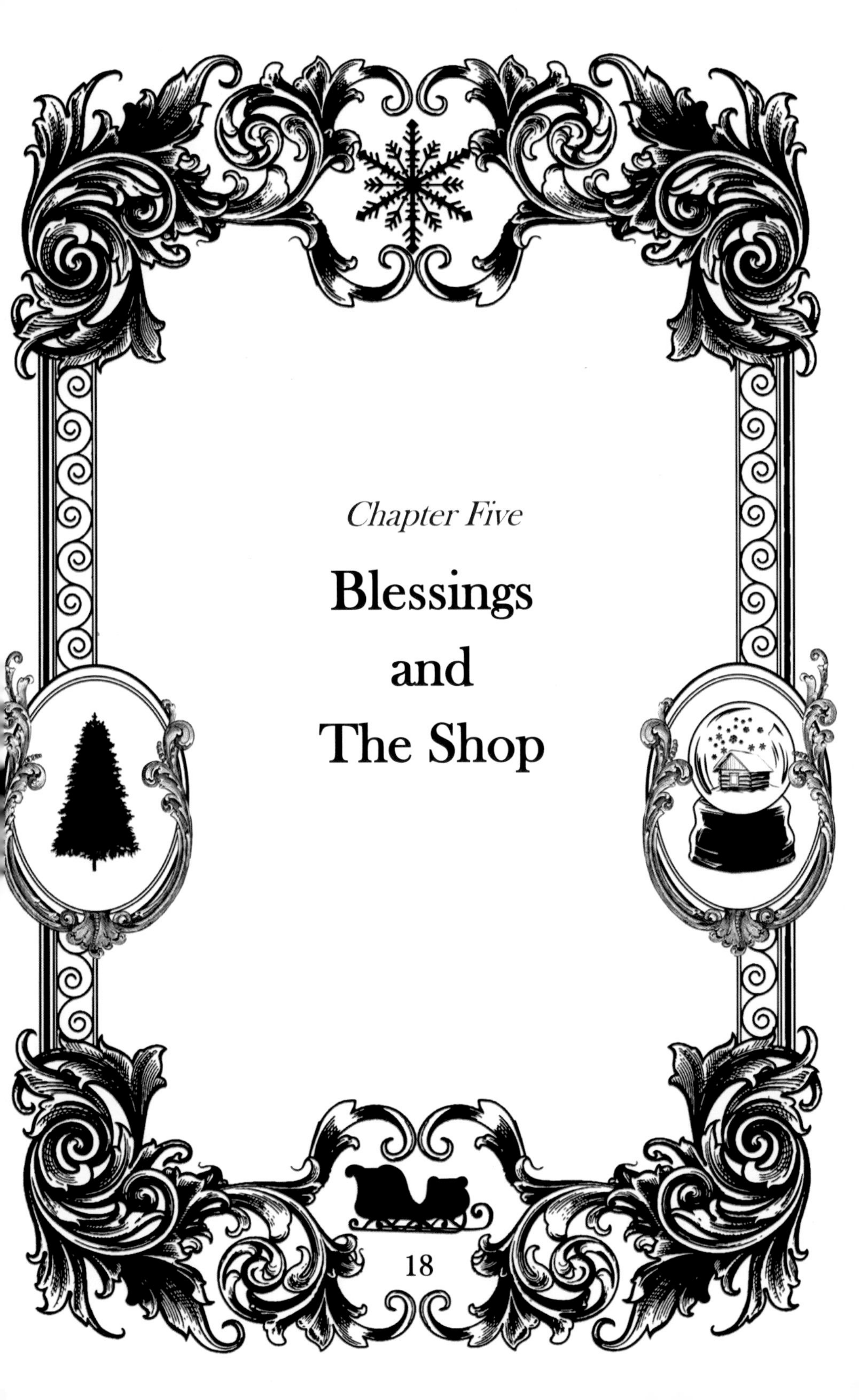

Chapter Five

Blessings and The Shop

They each took a turn to say
to the rest;
Of one thing to thank for, and
how they were blessed.

Blessed for their family who
sat all around;
Eating food at a table and not
on the ground.

For December, it was, and
cold to the bone;
And sad for the ones who
were eating alone.

They spoke of ideas to do
something good;
Until Nicholas chimed in and
said that he could.

"Tomorrow I visit a town in
despair;
I'll gather things here and
give while I'm there."

"I'll help you find more just
to put in your sleigh!"
Carol said with a grin as she
went on her way.

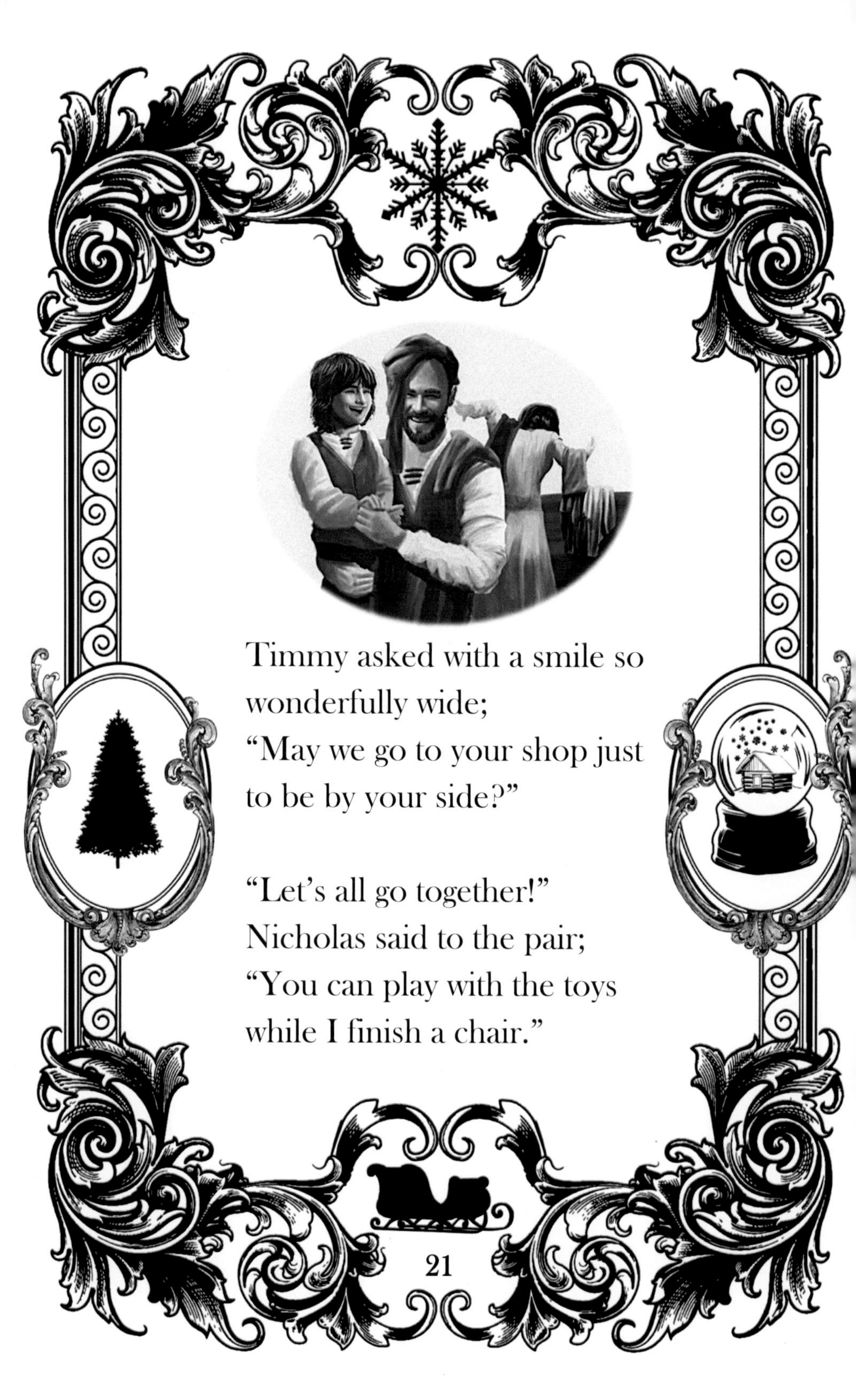

Timmy asked with a smile so
wonderfully wide;
"May we go to your shop just
to be by your side?"

"Let's all go together!"
Nicholas said to the pair;
"You can play with the toys
while I finish a chair."

Excited to go, they started to race;
And opened the door to their father's workplace.

They looked all around without making a noise;
At tables, and tools, and trinkets and toys.

Sculptures displayed and puppets that draped;
And plenty of items so beautifully shaped.

To Holly and Timmy each
visit was new;
As things came and went, and
quickly passed through.

The hour then chimed, and
they knew what that meant;
Their bedtime had come, so
inside they went.

"It's bedtime, you two!" their
father had said;
"Let's get you cleaned up and
off to your bed."

Nicholas and Carol then
tucked them in tight;
With a kiss and a hug, and a
loving "goodnight!"

PART TWO
"THE MAGIC IN THE EVE"

Chapter Six

The Next Morning

As rays from the sun broke
through the pine trees;
It warmed up the house with a
light winter breeze.

Even droplets of water that
fell from the ice;
Gave a noise that was soft
and sounded so nice.

The sounds all around woke
the children inside;
But the smell of baked goods
made their eyes open wide.

Excited to see what waited below;
The two little children were ready to go.

They hopped out of bed and ran down the stairs;
And wanted a hug with the strength of ten bears.

"Good morning, Mom!"
echoed the house all around;
But somewhere outside was
an all-familiar sound.

Their father was loading the
sleigh with his goods;
So off he could go through the
snow-covered woods.

They knew he wouldn't leave
without saying goodbye;
With his rosy-red cheeks and
a twinkle in his eye.

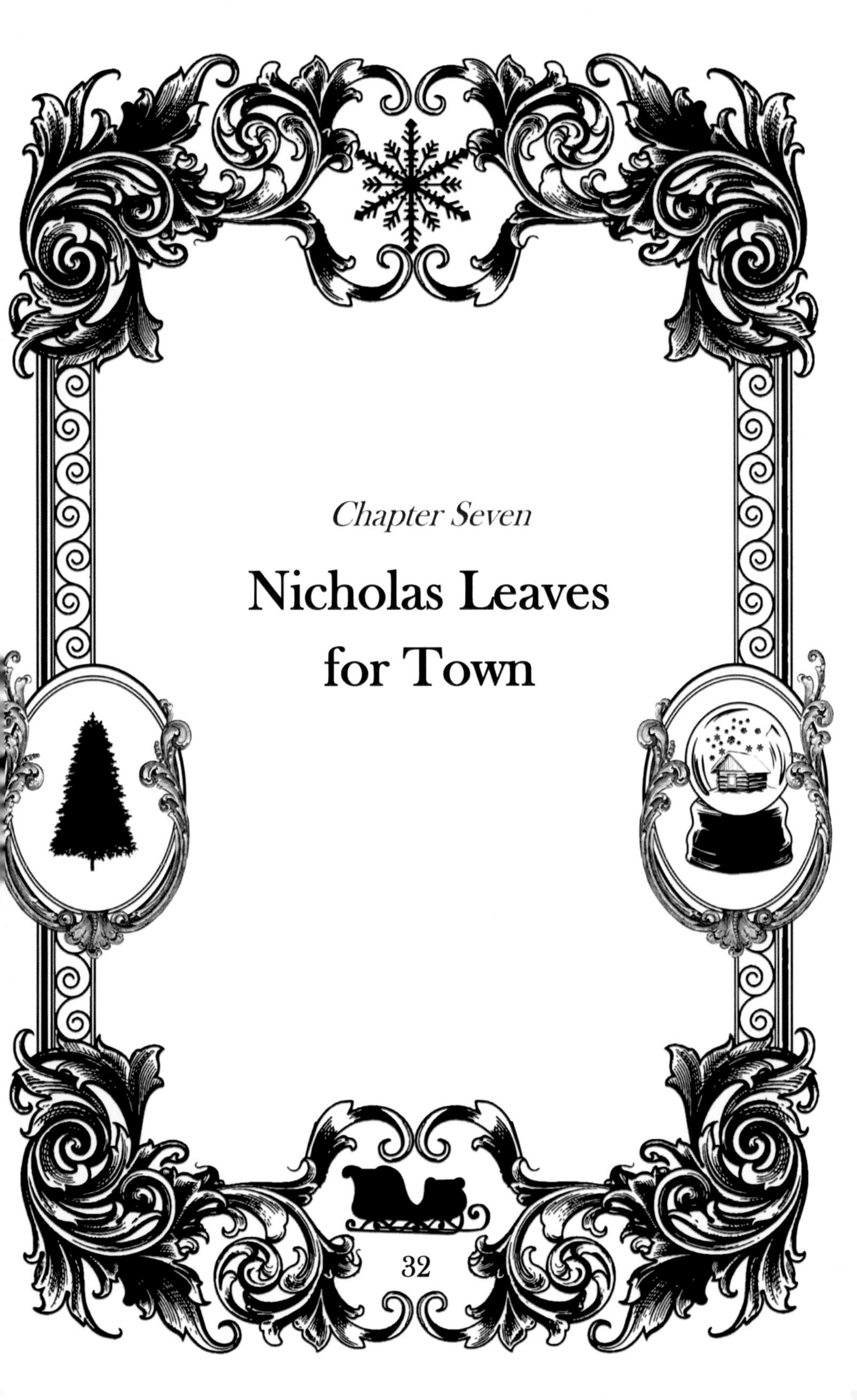

Chapter Seven

Nicholas Leaves for Town

He walked through the door
where his family awaits;
Along with a bag full of figs
and sweet dates.

Which Carol prepared for his
journey ahead;
As well as a loaf of her freshly-
baked bread.

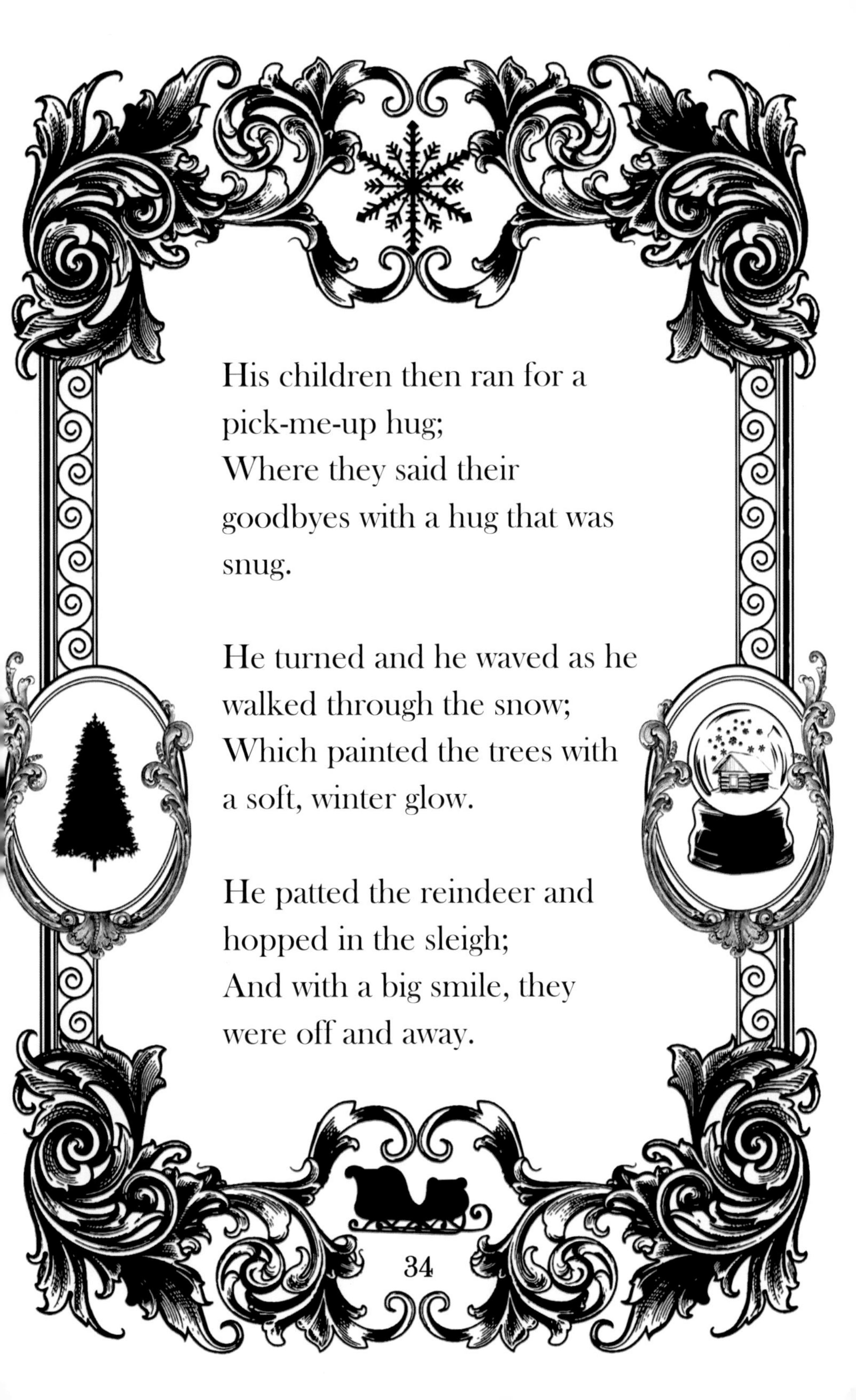

His children then ran for a
pick-me-up hug;
Where they said their
goodbyes with a hug that was
snug.

He turned and he waved as he
walked through the snow;
Which painted the trees with
a soft, winter glow.

He patted the reindeer and
hopped in the sleigh;
And with a big smile, they
were off and away.

The leather reins cracked and
the tension grew tight;
Then Nicholas and reindeer
were soon out of sight.

The journey was short for the
town was nearby;
They passed through low
valleys and mountains so high.

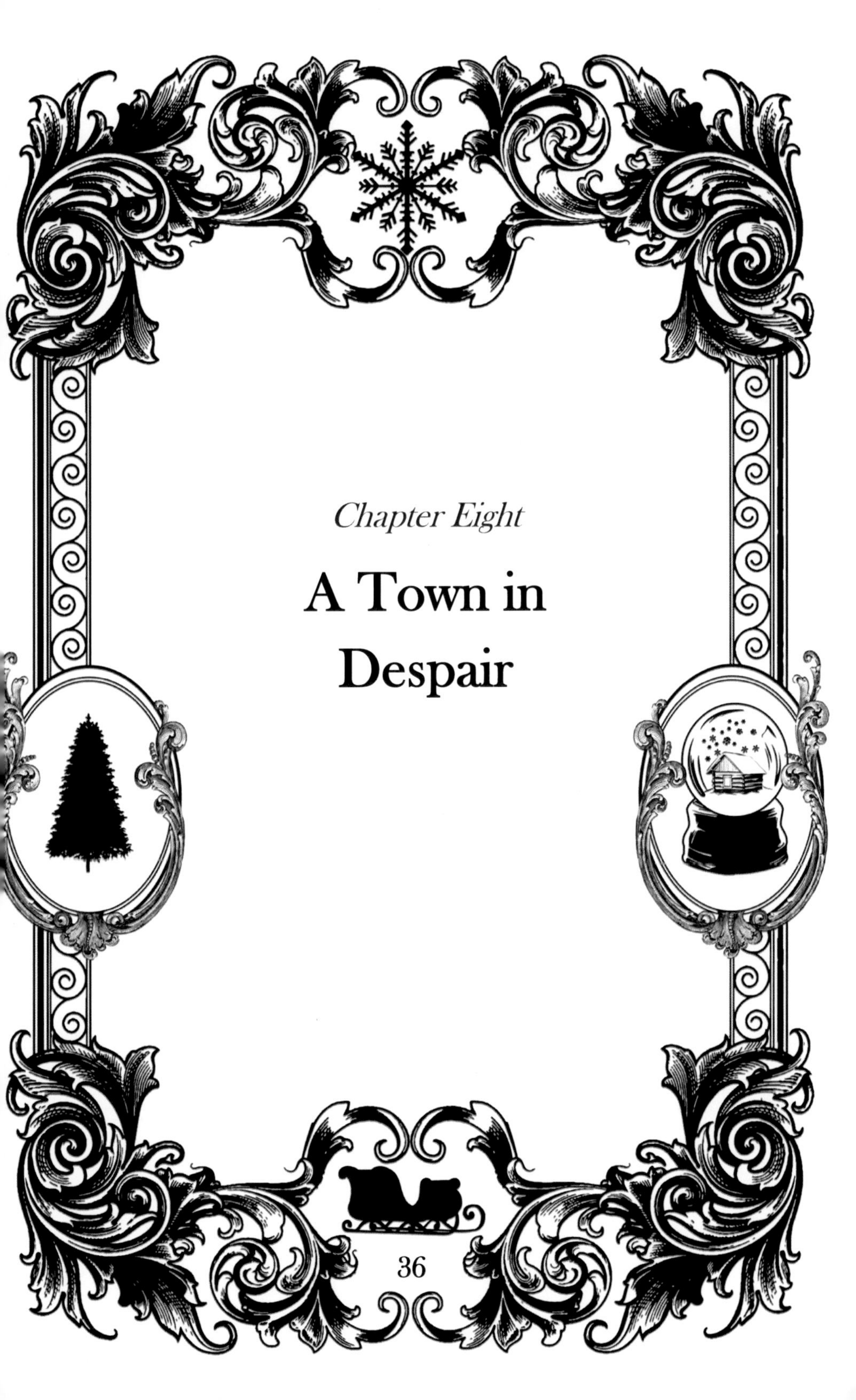

Chapter Eight

A Town in Despair

At last, they arrived to the center of town;
Which felt a bit cold and a little bit down.

It wasn't much time until he reached the first store;
Where he hopped out of the sleigh and knocked on the door.

A 'Knock, Knock, Knock!' came and he waited to see;
A man with his daughters...all one, two and three.

Greetings were said, and they walked to the sleigh;
Where they picked up their items and went on their way.

His trip would continue all over the town;
But he stopped when he saw someone pushed to the ground.

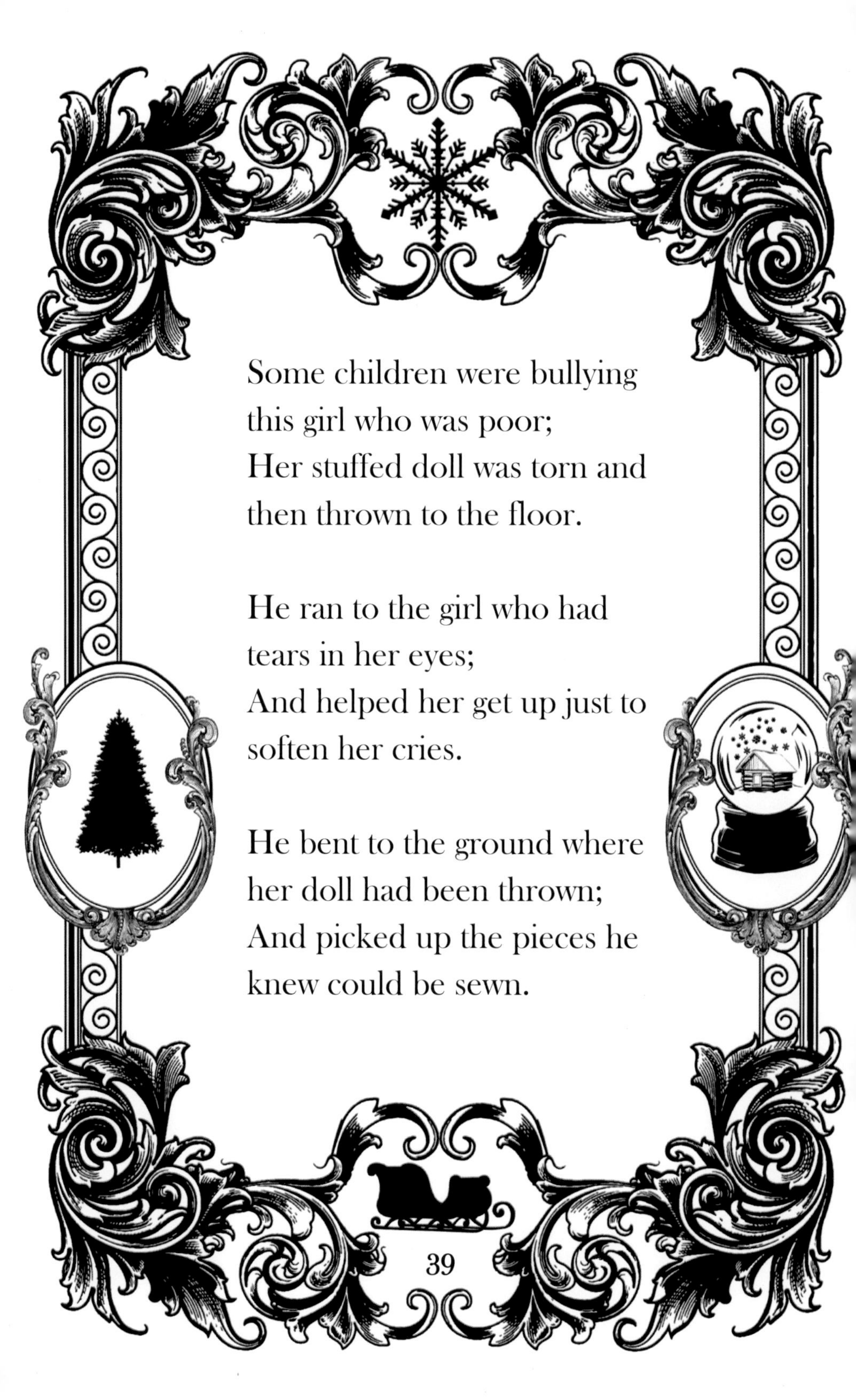

Some children were bullying
this girl who was poor;
Her stuffed doll was torn and
then thrown to the floor.

He ran to the girl who had
tears in her eyes;
And helped her get up just to
soften her cries.

He bent to the ground where
her doll had been thrown;
And picked up the pieces he
knew could be sewn.

"Don't worry, my dear! I'll
make it like new;
You'll have it right back in a
moment or two."

Chapter Nine

Meeting Mary

He walked to the sleigh and
pulled out of his bag;
A needle, some thread, and a
plum-colored rag.

Then out came some magic
and the doll was together;
Even adding a scarf just to
fight off the weather.

He brought the doll back to
the girl who stood by;
And she was happy to see it,
by the look in her eye.

"What is your name?" he
asked her politely;
"Mary." she whispered ever so
lightly.

This girl was in need, as
Nicholas could see;
For clothing and food, or a
hot cup of tea.

So, he went to his sleigh and
he packed a bag full;
Of bread and some clothes
that were made out of wool.

Her eyes became large, like a
full moon at night;
And a smile to fill up a dark
room with light.

"Thank you! Oh, thank you!"
she said in reply;
And Mary, too excited, had
started to cry.

But Nicholas was happy, for
he knew that those cries;
Were not from a pain, but of
joy in disguise.

Chapter Ten

Coal and Two More Reindeer

He then had to leave to finish his chores;
To walk the town's streets and sell to more stores.

He walked and he walked on the uneven brick;
But stopped when he saw someone raising a stick.

He looked at two reindeer
who appeared to be hurt;
They were battered and
bruised and covered in dirt.

"Stop what you're doing! I'll
give what you need;
I'll purchase your reindeer…I
beg and I plead!"

And after much talk, an
arrangement was made;
That he'd do what he could,
no matter how much he paid.

He gathered the two and
walked toward the sleigh;
And did so with haste and
without delay.

But as they were walking, it
broke to his soul;
Just how these two lived with
a miner of coal.

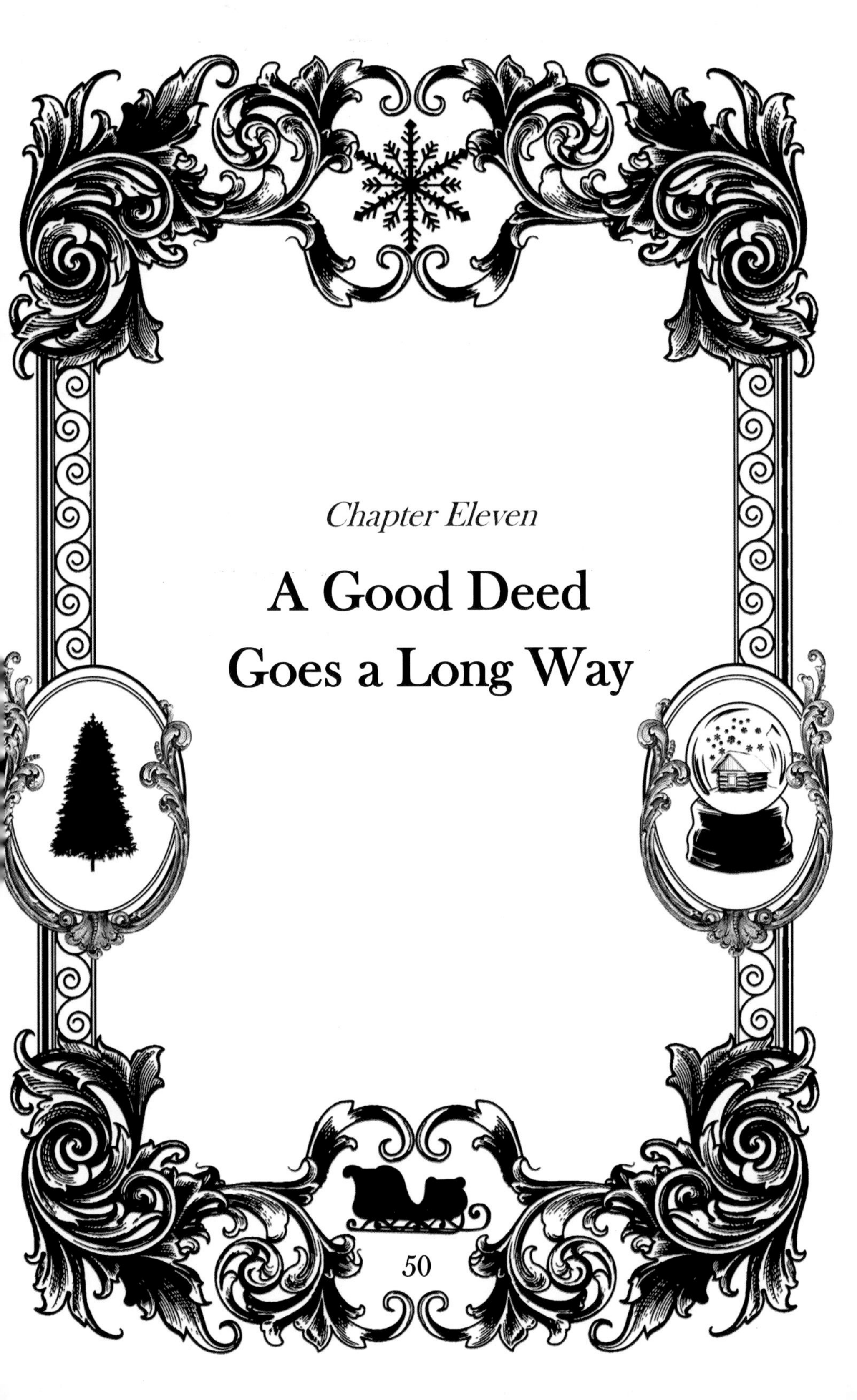

Chapter Eleven

A Good Deed Goes a Long Way

As he brought the two
reindeer where the others had
waited;
He saw little Mary by a park
that was gated.

He then saw a man who paid
her no mind;
Not knowing his coin bag was
soon to unwind.

No care for the girl and the
poor life she knew;
To him she was dirt on the
bottom of his shoe.

And then his bag fell to
Mary's poor feet;
As Nicholas stood watching
from across the stone street.

He expected to see her just
take it and go;
But what he saw next made
his heart start to grow.

Mary called to the man whose
coins fell to the floor;
And he stopped, and he
turned, not knowing what for.

The man was in awe but a
"Huff!" was his praise;
As he tossed her some coins
and went back to his ways.

Nicholas was curious and
crossed the stone street;
Now wanting to know why
she'd acted so sweet.

"That was nice what you did!"
he said with delight;
"That your action was good
and not out of spite."

Her response was *as* good, for
he didn't expect;
That it came from a life,
which was filled with reject.

"I was taught not to take even
though I am poor;
Like helping that man whose
coins fell to the floor."

Astonished and awed, he gave
her a smile;
And said that her actions were
more than worthwhile.

"I'm sorry to go, but my
family now waits;
But please take this small bag,
which is filled with some
dates."

He waved a goodbye and
walked toward the sleigh;
Then him and four reindeer
were off and away.

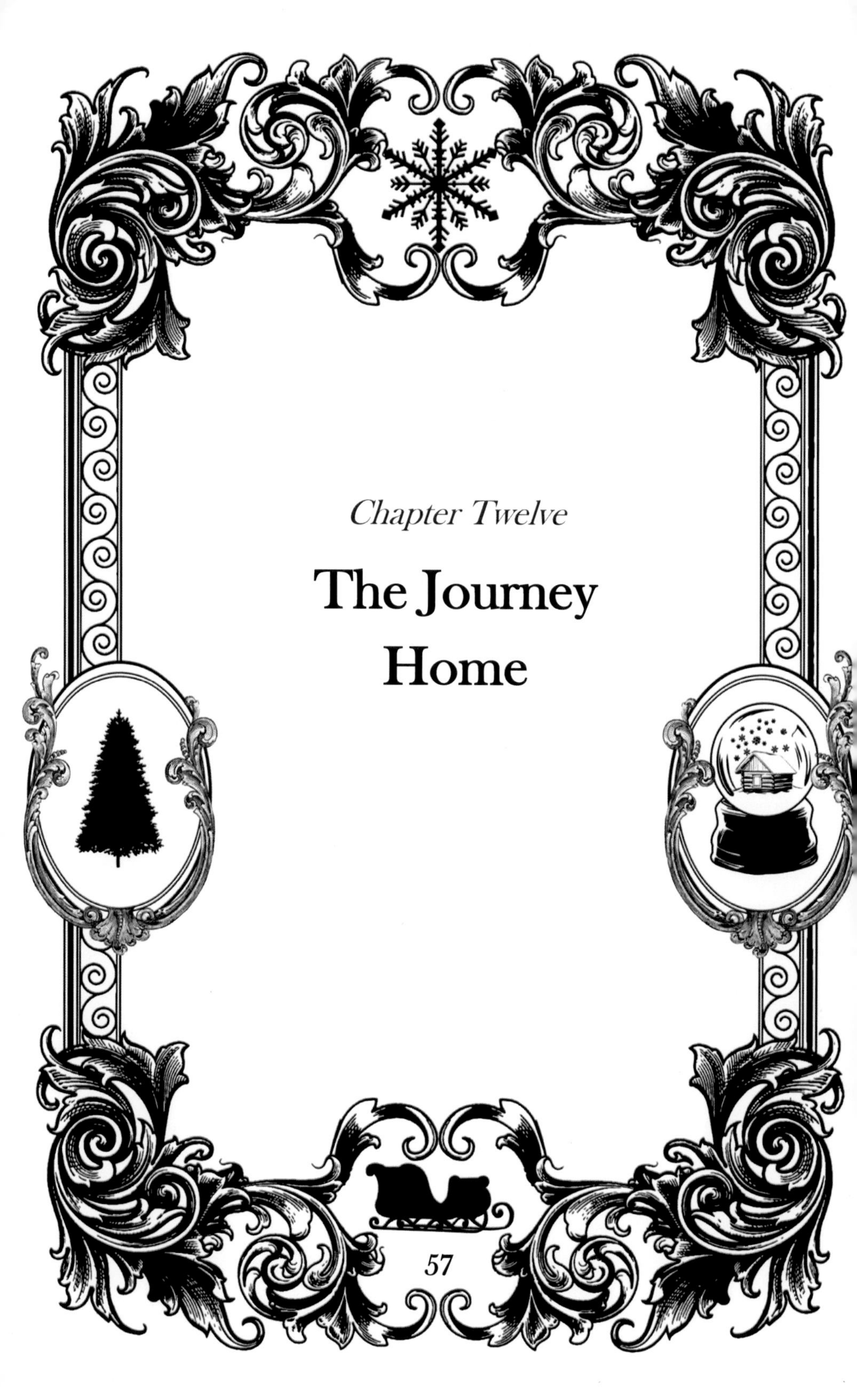

Chapter Twelve

The Journey Home

He threw up his hood just to
fight off the nip;
While he reached for the
reins and tightened his grip.

It was during his travels he
remembered he'd forgot;
To name the two reindeer he
recently bought.

"Blitzen and Comet!" he
quickly cheered out;
For something had told him
those names would stand out.

Then out of the dark, his
house came in sight;
From several small windows
that glowed in the night.

He guided four reindeer to
the comfortable shed;
And tucked them in tight in
their soft, cozy beds.

He walked to the sleigh just to
grab what's in back;
Expecting to find just an
empty red sac.

But something *was* there,
laying just out-of-sight;
And something he'd find
later on in the night.

He entered the shop and
placed the bag down;
Recalling the day and that
poor little town.

The night went by quick, filled
with food and some fun;
With toys and an act played
by daughter and son.

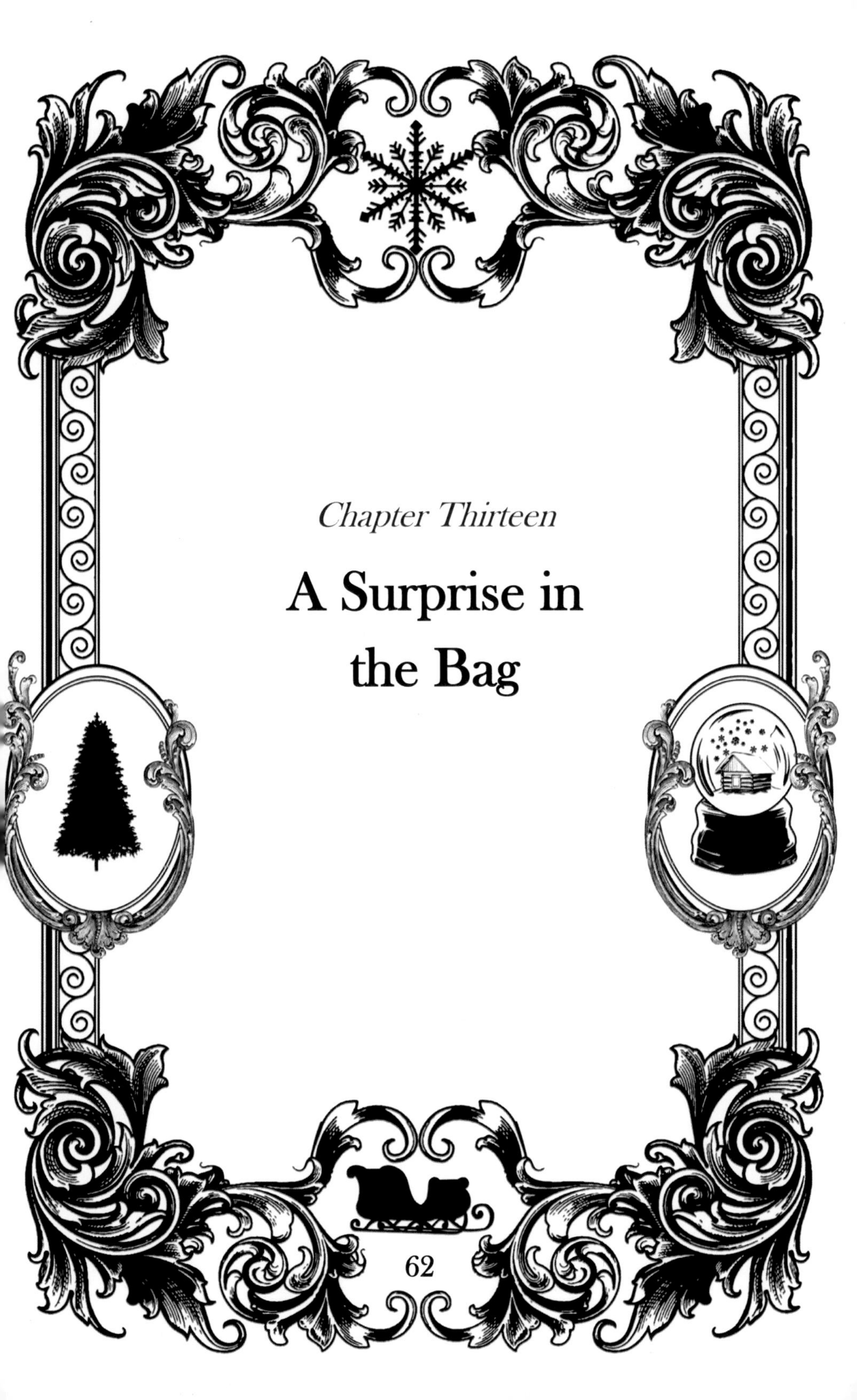

Chapter Thirteen

A Surprise in the Bag

Carol then nestled in a chair
where she read;
While Holly and Timmy fell
asleep in their bed.

Nicholas walked to the shop
just to clean for the night;
Where he opened the door to
a room filled with light.

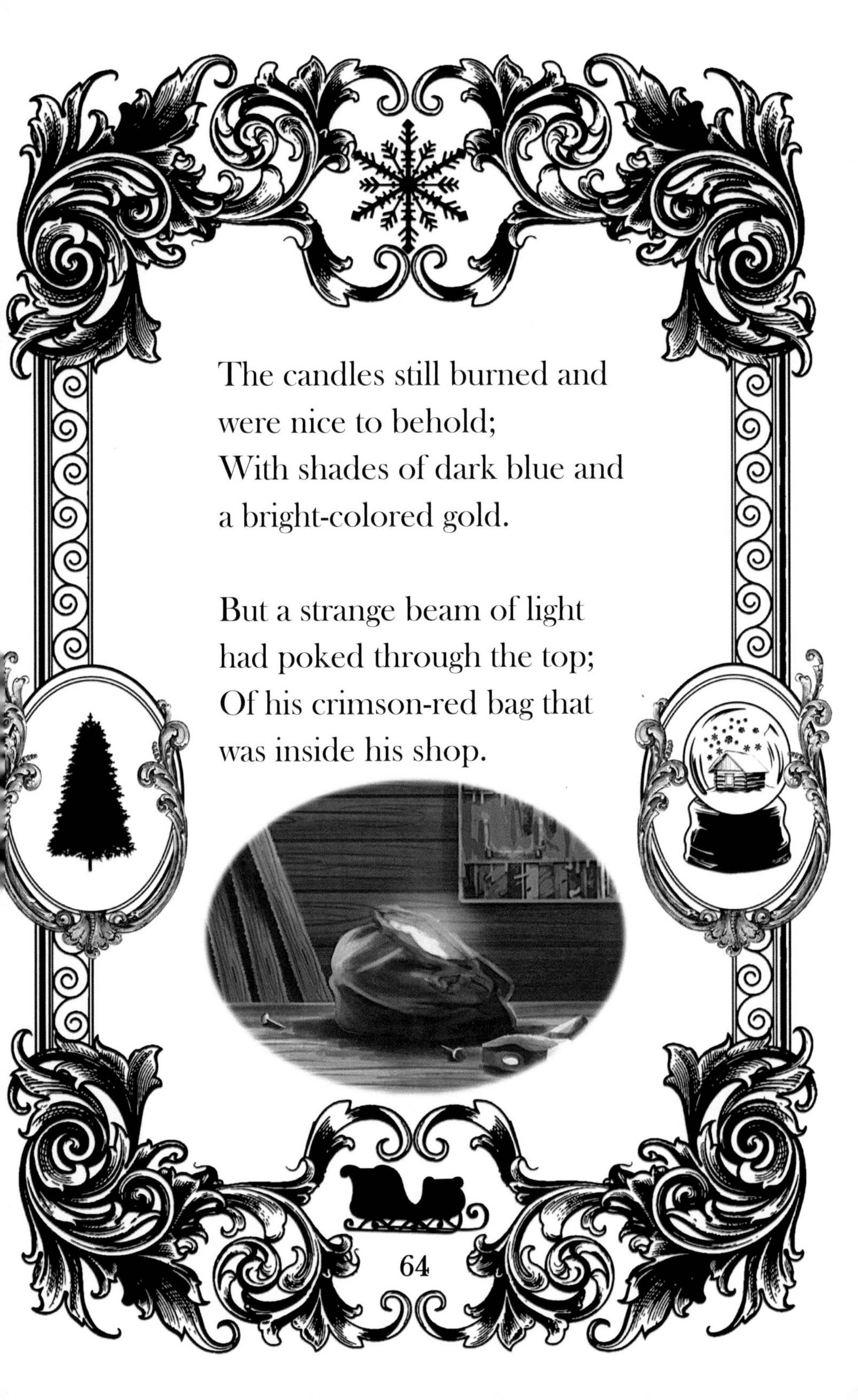

The candles still burned and
were nice to behold;
With shades of dark blue and
a bright-colored gold.

But a strange beam of light
had poked through the top;
Of his crimson-red bag that
was inside his shop.

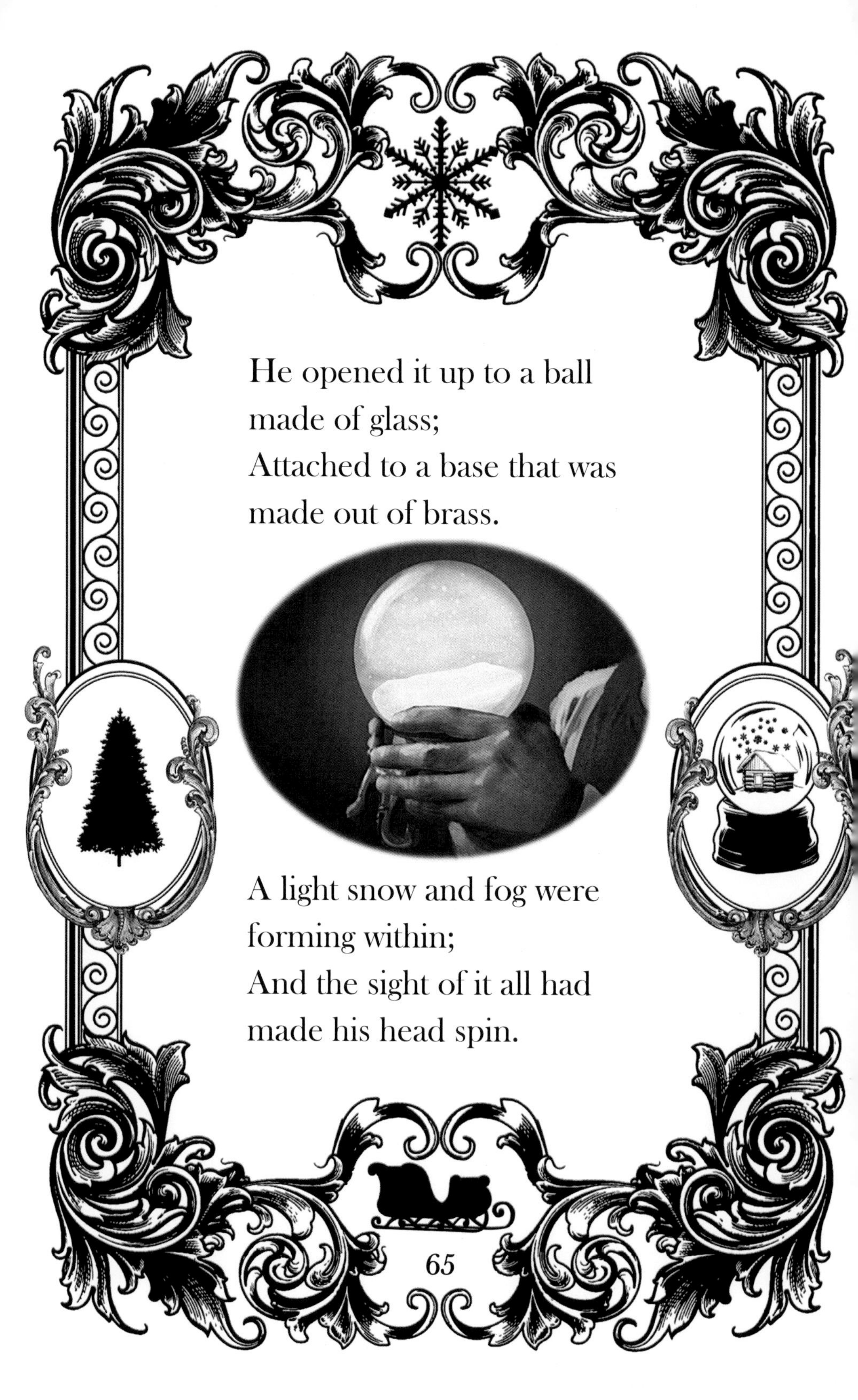

He opened it up to a ball
made of glass;
Attached to a base that was
made out of brass.

A light snow and fog were
forming within;
And the sight of it all had
made his head spin.

It faded away to something he knew;
A fireless fireplace had slowly come through.

Then a handful of coal was next to be seen;
Which gave little heat that could warm anything.

And then out of nowhere a
family arose;
Surrounding this “warmth” in
their ragged, old clothes.

The total was six, and they
snuggled so tight;
Four boys and two girls had
surrounded the light.

The mother was holding some bread for them all;
It seemed to be dinner...but *awfully* small.

The mother broke it in pieces and passed it around;
While they sat by the coal and ate on the ground.

As Nicholas was watching this heartbreaking view;
He noticed the girl...it was someone he knew.

"That's Mary!" he said as she grabbed her small slice;
And broke it in half...without thinking twice.

She handed it over to the smallest of all;
Who sat next to her and their broken-down wall.

He looked to be weak and
shivered too much;
Unable to walk without
holding a crutch.

A tear hit the globe while
Nicholas looked on;
Then a second one hit and
everything was gone.

He held it up close as if to
compel;
A wish for this family and a
life to live well.

"I wish for some warmth,
some food, and some joy;
For that nice girl named Mary
to simply enjoy."

He didn't know why but
something felt real;
Not something to touch, but
something to feel.

He placed the globe down to finish the day;
And went straight to bed after loading his sleigh.

PART THREE
A DAY OF MIRACLES

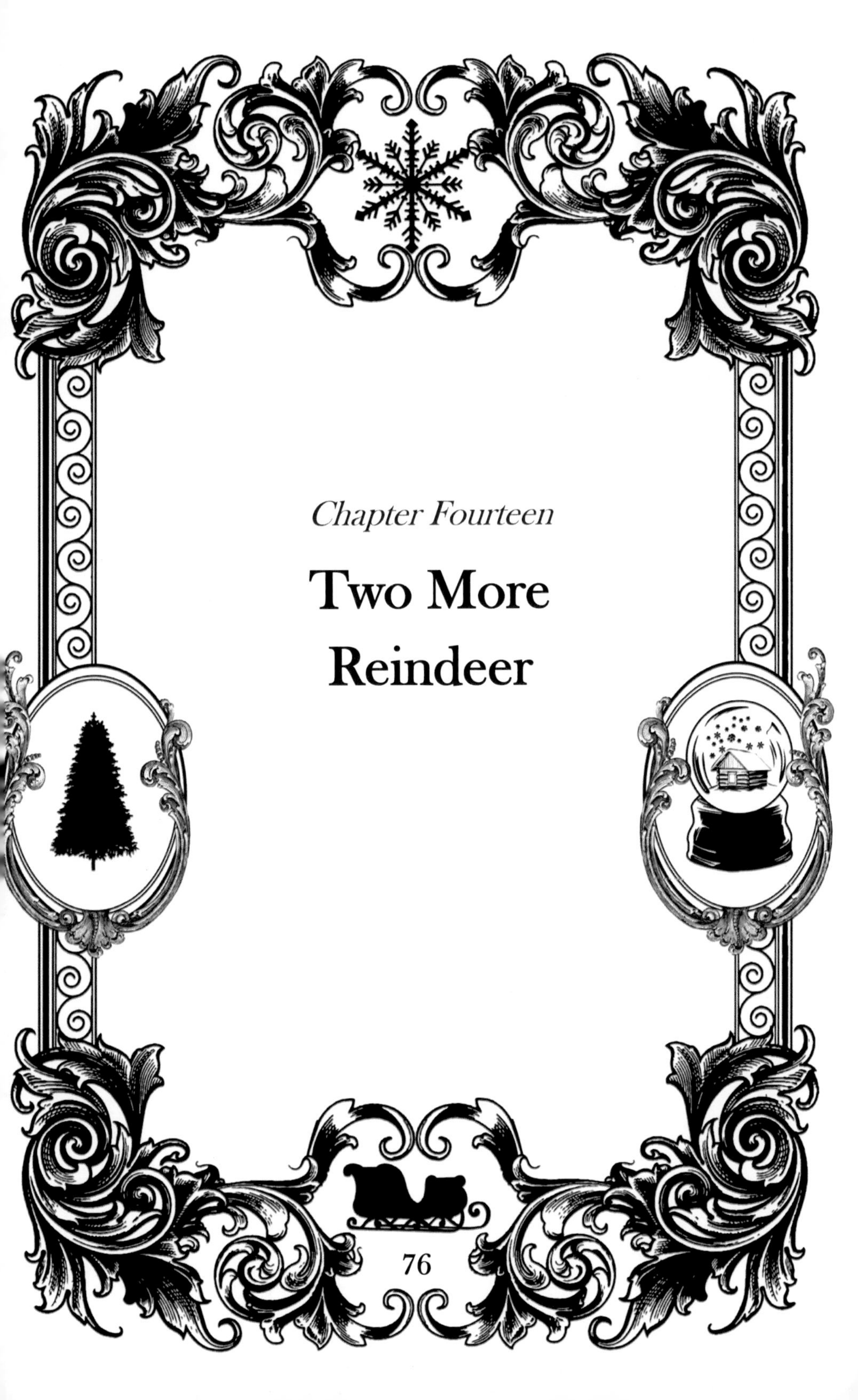

Chapter Fourteen

Two More Reindeer

A new day had come and the
sun would soon rise;
But Nicholas and all would get
a surprise.

Loud noises and yelps were
heard just outside;
A reindeer was stuck with one
by its side.

It was caught in some
branches, no way to get free;
While the other had stayed by
the trunk of a tree.

Nicholas hurried to help
without giving them fright;
Then the reindeer was free
and he pranced with delight.

No sign of a father or even
their mother;
Once he realized these two
were sister and brother.

“I have a nice home, if you
two want to stay;
You’ll have a nice family and
food every day.”

He walked toward the barn
and noticed the two;
Were following behind at the
heel of his shoe.

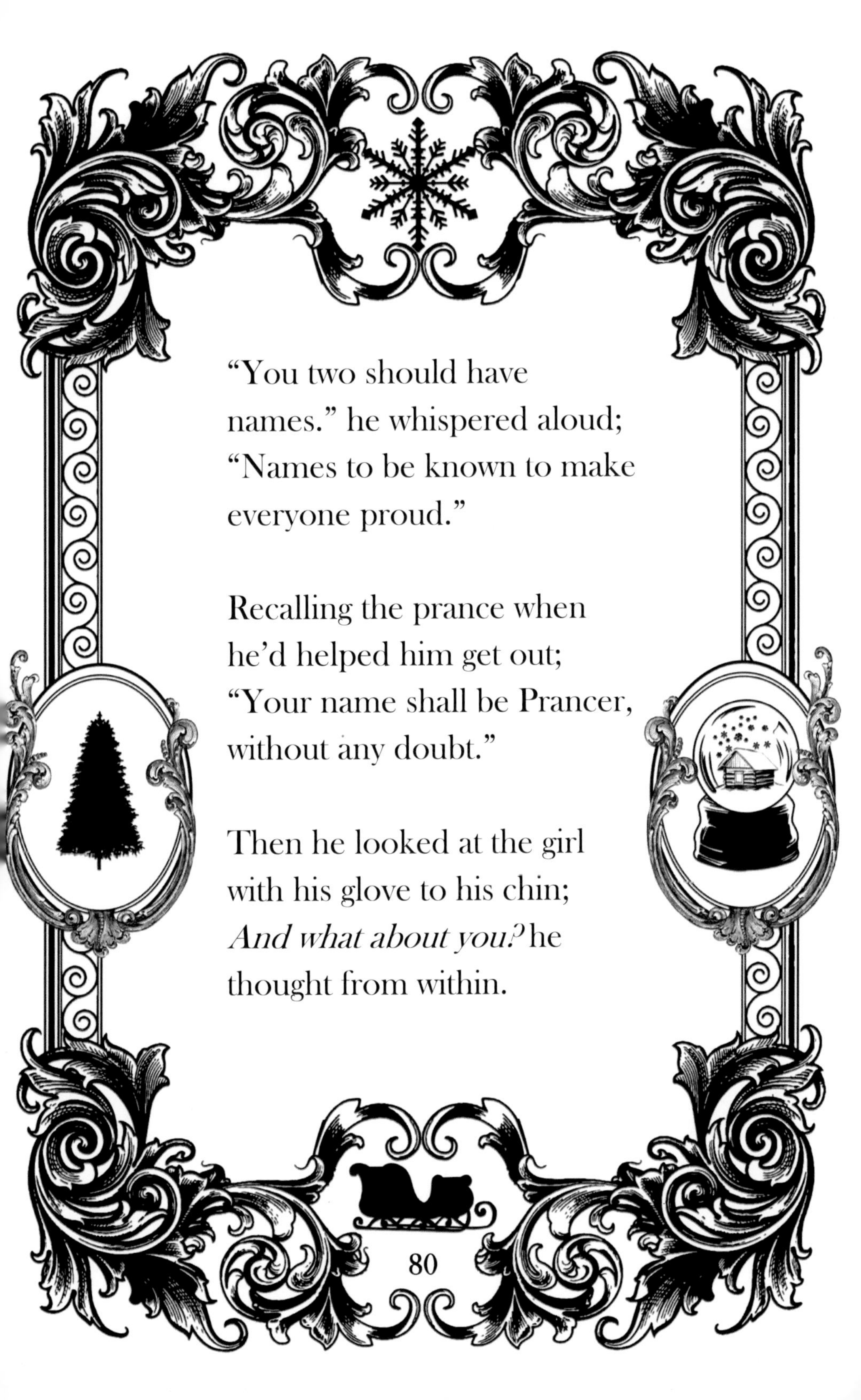

"You two should have
names." he whispered aloud;
"Names to be known to make
everyone proud."

Recalling the prance when
he'd helped him get out;
"Your name shall be Prancer,
without any doubt."

Then he looked at the girl
with his glove to his chin;
And what about you? he
thought from within.

You cared for your brother,
all stuck and entwined;
He thought...and he thought...
then Cupid came to mind.

"I *was* hit by your arrow,
which went to my heart;
And I feel like you two can
play a big part."

And now, with six reindeer
inside of the shed;
Nicholas got them some water
and readied his sled.

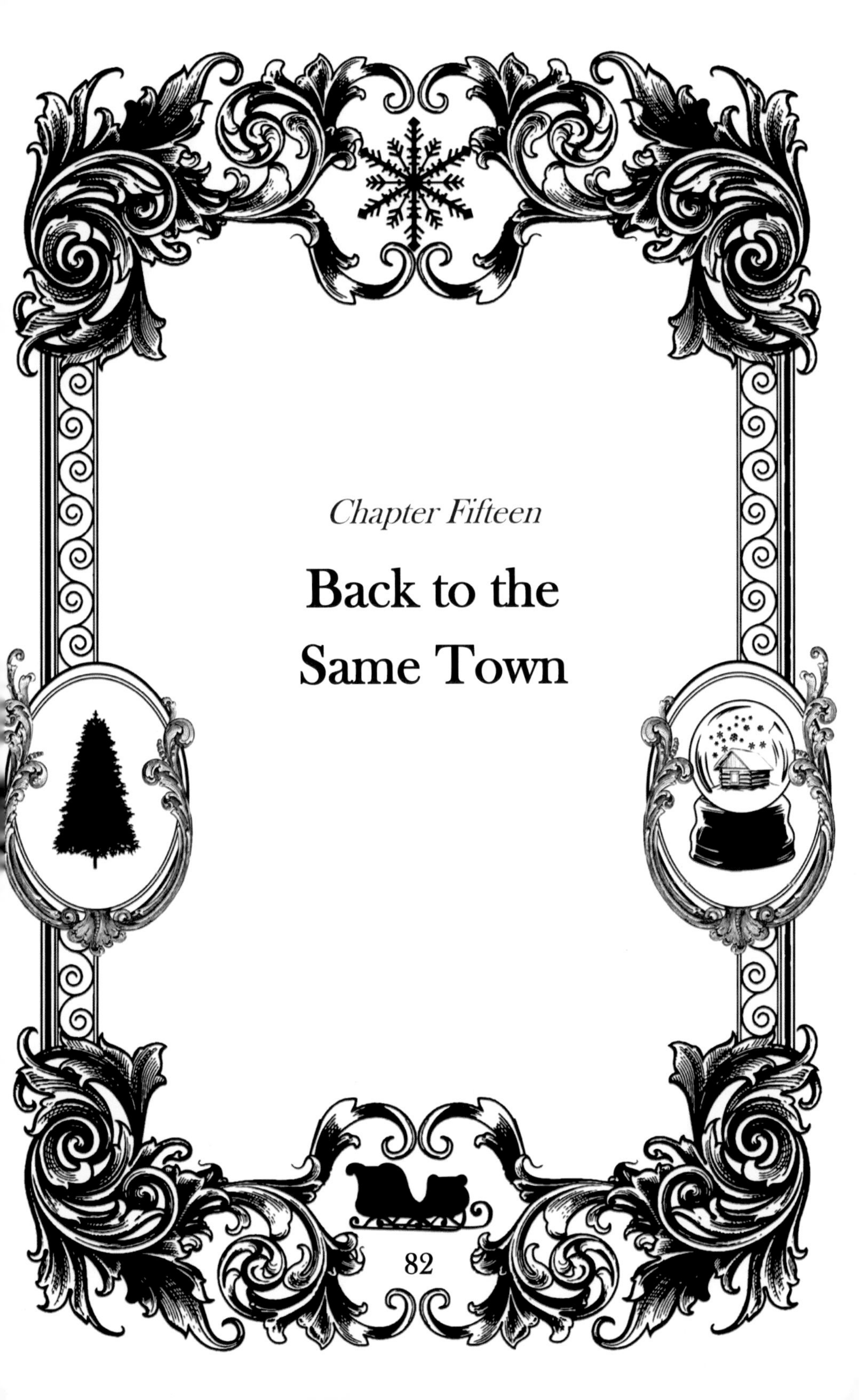

Chapter Fifteen

Back to the Same Town

He walked in the house, for
one final thing;
A bag he'd prepared and
wanted to bring.

"I thought you had left," Carol
said with surprise;
"but I'm happy you're back
with those lovely, blue eyes.

"I thought you had missed
that small bag over there;"
Carol pointed her finger to a
spot by the chair.

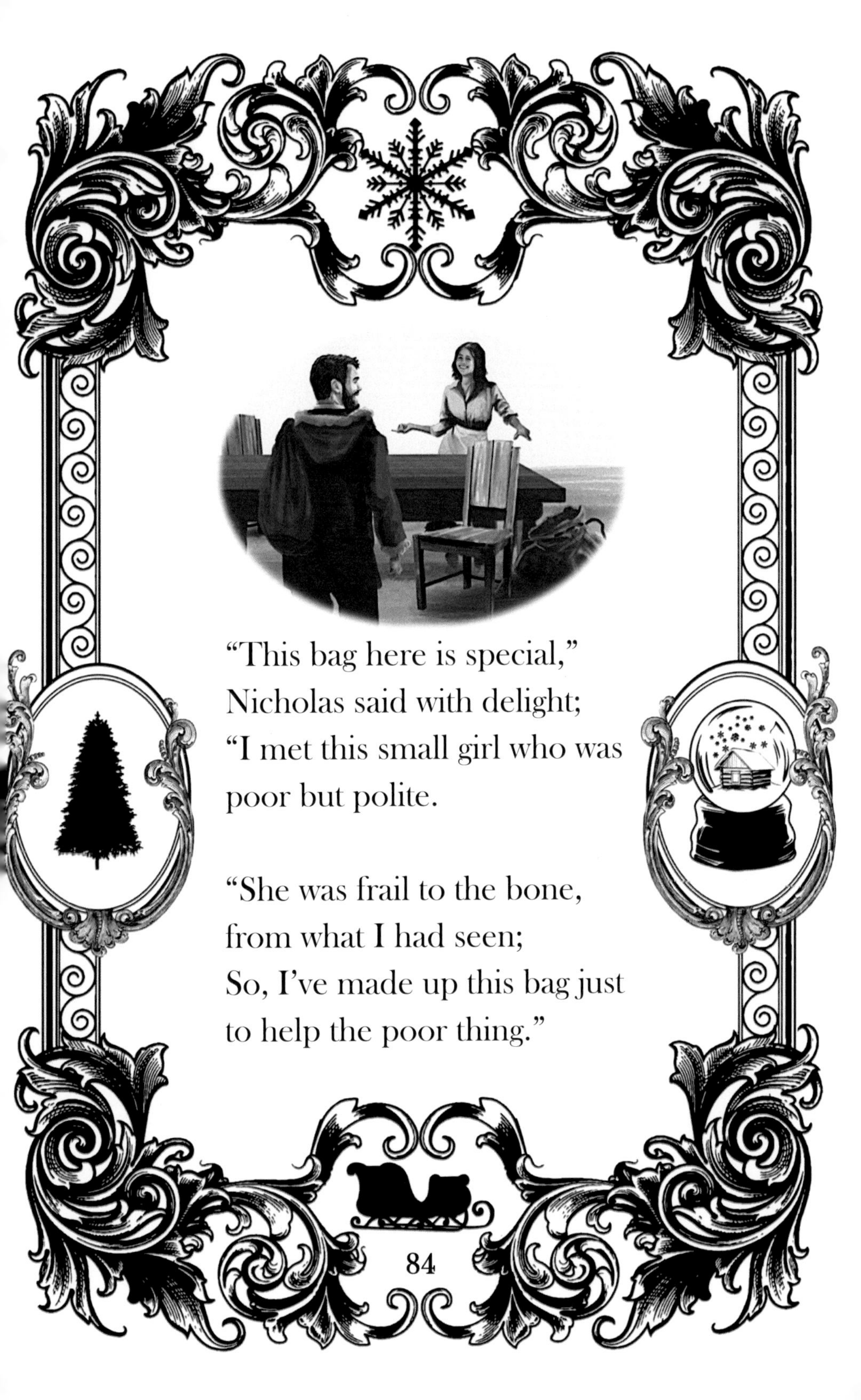

"This bag here is special,"
Nicholas said with delight;
"I met this small girl who was
poor but polite.

"She was frail to the bone,
from what I had seen;
So, I've made up this bag just
to help the poor thing."

Carol left in a hurry and said
she'll be back;
With more things to add to
his gifts in the sac.

Blankets and clothes were all
she could carry;
But what she had heard left
her joyful and merry.

"Take these," she said "and
get on your way;
It's already late and you
mustn't delay."

The reindeer were ready and
tied to the sleigh;
Nicholas hopped in his seat
and was off and away.

And much like before, the
journey was brief;
And he made it to town
without any grief.

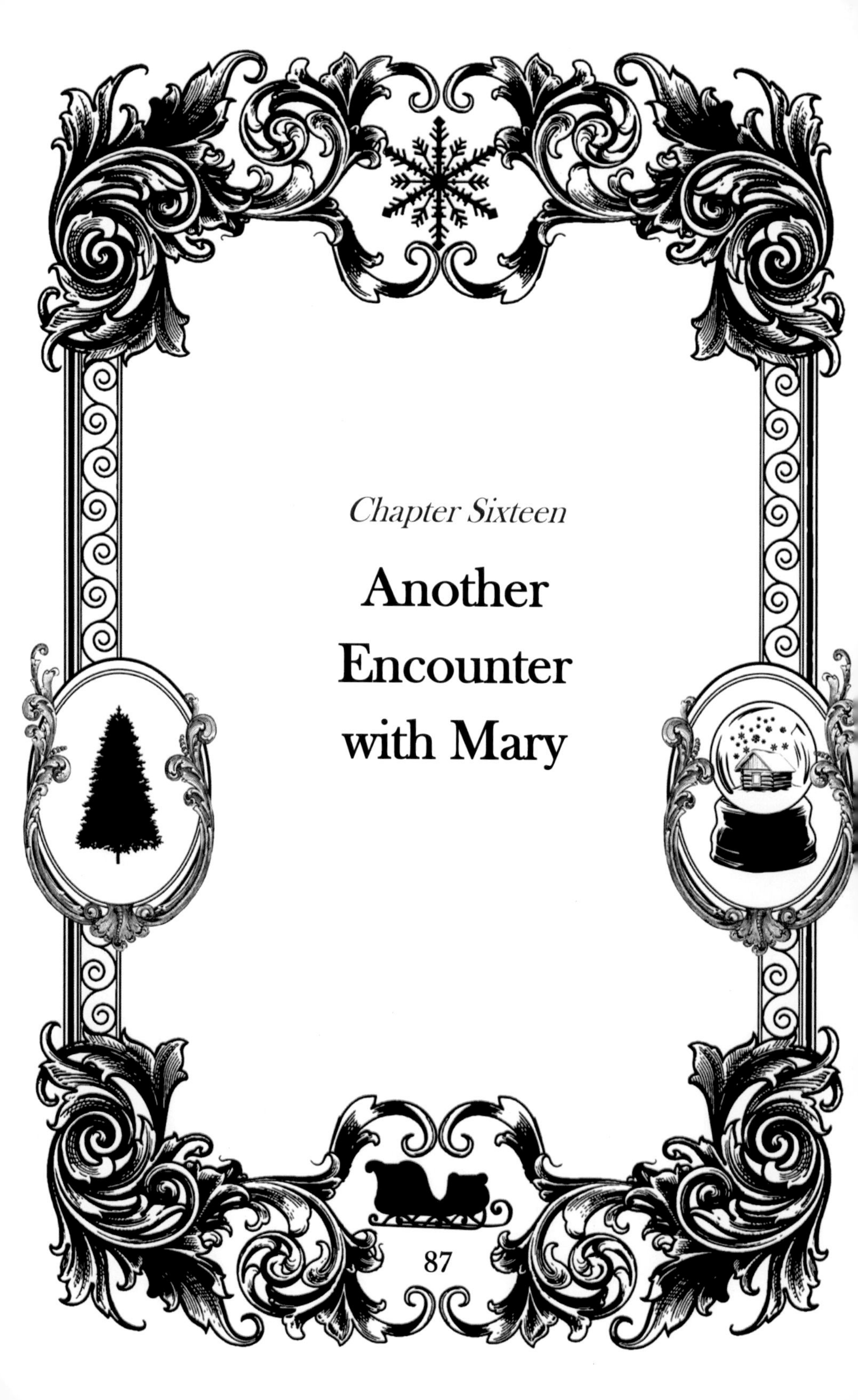

Chapter Sixteen

Another Encounter with Mary

He looked to the spot where
Mary had sat;
But all he could see was a
small alley cat.

With no sign of Mary, he
walked up the street;
To a bakery nearby, for
something to eat.

It wasn't too far from his
reindeer and sleigh;
"It smells so delicious!" was all
he could say.

He picked up some cookies,
some bread, and spiced meat;
Then left the warm store for
his sleigh on the street.

As he loaded the sleigh, he saw with delight;
That little girl Mary, so lively and bright.

She walked to the corner with a skip in her feet;
Dragging one handsome bag that was made from a sheet.

When she looked toward his
way, she shouted “Hello!”
Her words and her smile
made his heart start to grow.

He waved in return while he
started to lift;
The bag in his sleigh that was
meant as a gift.

“Mary!” he said, “I have this
for you!”
She jumped and she jumped
with a cheerful “Thank you!”

He laid the bag down and
walked toward the sleigh;
Happy to know she was
smiling today.

As he hopped in his sleigh, he
saw with surprise;
Mary running around with
affection in her eyes.

She ran all around with the
blankets and food;
To children and grownups, to
brighten their mood.

Then Nicholas just sat there
with nothing to say;
As he watched little Mary give
his gifts all away.

"Mary?!" he asked as he
walked toward her way;
Curious to know if she's
feeling okay.

"These things were for you...is
everything all right?"
But her response was a story
of her magical night.

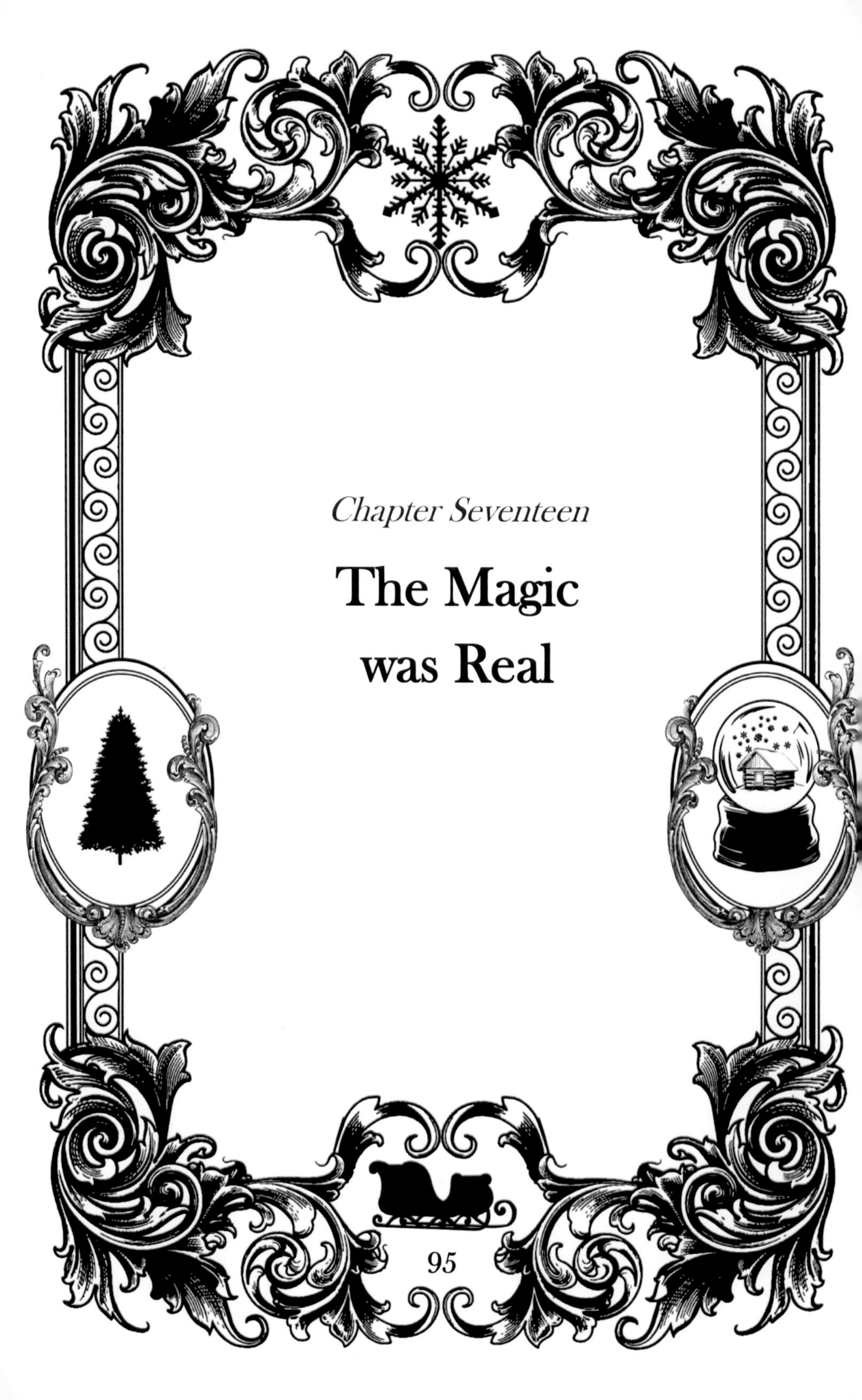

Chapter Seventeen

The Magic was Real

"We woke to a room, which was filled with all things;
Of clothes, food and coins...enough for three Kings!

Colorful clothes and toys everywhere;
Warm food and bright silver found here and found there.

The shouts from my brothers
had shook the whole house;
But Joseph, the youngest, was
as quiet as a mouse.

Speechless, he was, but happy
indeed;
And looking around, we all
had agreed.

Last night we had bread,
which broke to our soul;
It was split between six, all
huddled by coal.

We had no idea that we'd
wake to a room;
Which warmed up our hearts
when all had seemed gloom."

Nicholas thought of the globe
he had seen from last night;
If that magic, and wish, had
come true overnight.

Did all of this happen? he
thought to himself;
*Or was it a visit by some magic
elf?*

Convinced of this miracle
from what Mary just said;
This globe *was* a blessing to
what lay ahead.

And as he was thinking, Mary
snuck right away;
To give out more gifts on this
magical day.

Chapter Eighteen

A New Future Begins

He turned to a store that sold
many things;
And bought more and more
for this angel with wings.

All placed in a bag, he walked
back to Mary;
Who danced round and
round like a little snow fairy.

The bag was then placed on
the snow-covered ground;
And he quietly left without
making a sound.

He walked to the sleigh, now
happy to know;
Mary spotted his gift that was
left in the snow.

Her smile was large with his
gifts laid about;
But what he saw next seemed
to *really* stand out.

She ran all around with what
she could hold;
Giving everything she had to
the young and the old.

But *what* seemed to shine was
what happened next;
To the people she gave to,
and all its effects.

For more and more gave to
those all around;
Which brightened the mood
of this once-darkened town.

And in that split moment, he
took it all in;
The love and respect, and the
giving within.

He named this whole moment
that made his heart merry;
Of gifts that were given by a
sweet girl named Mary.

This day had now changed,
and it was easy to see;
It was greater than Nicholas,
and "Mary's Christmas" came
to be.

Coal

Afterword

First and foremost, thank you for reading the story about Nicholas and how it all began.

It was designed to imitate The Telephone Game – a fun game where you and a group of friends sit in a circle, one person makes up a short sentence, and is repeated (...either once or twice) to your neighbor in a way so that nobody else can hear. The interesting part of the game is if the original sentence can stay the same around the whole circle, or it's completely changed by the time it returns back to the person who first said it.

The spirit meant to be expressed within this book is one I feel should be spread to as many people out there. If you feel the same, please provide a review or spread this manner of kindness to as many people out there.

This book would never have been made if it weren't for the medical staff at Walter Reed National Military Medical Center. Surviving two comas and brain surgery has profoundly opened my eyes to a new way of life. If you'd like to read more about the story, please visit my website at www.kylepoehls.com to get an in-depth story at of an experience which changed my life. Twice I lived through several hundred seizures with a 24-hour period and was able to live to tell the tale of this horrific experience in survival.

Again, thank you for allowing me to take you on this journey through time and the origin of traditions. This is the beginning of a new way to look at this holiday season.